LOCKWOOD
LIONS

The Lockwood High cheer squad has it *all*—sass, looks, and all the right moves. But everything isn't always as perfect as it seems. Because where there's cheer, there's drama. And then there are the ballers—hot, tough, and on point. But what's going to win out—life's pressures or their NFL dreams?

CHEER Drama

Sweetheart Ella Blount will do anything
to keep her girls together ...
...anything.

YELL OUT

Stephanie Perry Moore

SADDLEBACK
EDUCATIONAL PUBLISHING

CHEER DRAMA

Always Upbeat

Keep Jumping

Yell Out

Settle Down

Shake It

SADDLEBACK
EDUCATIONAL PUBLISHING
www.sdlback.com

ISBN-13: 978-1-61651-886-8
ISBN-10: 1-61651-886-3
eBook: 978-1-61247-620-9

Printed in Guangzhou, China
0612/CA21200872

16 15 14 13 12   1 2 3 4 5

To Marjorie Kimbrough (my mentor), Lakeba Williams (my accountability partner), and Tiffani Mischelle (mentee)

You all keep me grounded and whole. I really am thankful I have each of you in my life. Keep on yelling in life with me. Your time, heart, and love inspires me to shout for joy that my life has purpose. May every reader live to make folks around them better and always seek to be better themselves.

Stay connected with me … I love you!

ACKNOWLEDGEMENTS

It is hard to sit on the sidelines and do nothing when you see wrong things happening before your very eyes. You want to be the difference maker. You do not want to sit idly by and watch things go awry. You want to make things better for those you care about.

But taking a stand is not always easy. Sometimes when you have a big heart, folks take advantage. Sometimes you don't want to hurt people's feelings, so you do not call them out on their wrongs. However, when you don't dig deep and find the voice inside of you that shouts for truth, then you are letting yourself down. In other words … stand for what is right at all costs and do not be pushed around.

Here is a gargantuan thank you to everyone who helps me scream nuggets of truth in my novels.

For my parents, Dr. Franklin and Shirley Perry Sr., thanks for your voice that daily told me positive things to help me grow with self esteem.

Acknowledgements

For my publisher, especially my editor, Carol Pizer, thanks for your wonderful words of encouragement about my writing that keeps me feeling like I do have something to offer.

For my extended family: brother, Dennis Perry, mother-in-law, Ann Redding, brother-in-Christ, Jay Spencer, and goddaughter Danielle Lynn, thanks for your support that keeps me smiling since I have great folks in my corner.

For my assistants: Joy Spencer and Keisha King, thanks, ladies, for being a good sport and allowing me to shout at you so we could make our deadlines.

For my friends who are dear to my heart: Leslie Perry, Sarah Lundy, Jenell Clark, Nicole Smith, Jackie Dixon, Torian Colon, Loni Perriman, Kim Forest, Vickie Davis, Kim Monroe, Jamell Meeks, Michele Jenkins, Lois Barney, Veronica Evans, Laurie Weaver, Taiwanna Brown-Bolds, Matosha Glover, Yolanda Rodgers-Howsie, Dayna Fleming, Denise Gilmore, and Deborah Bradley, thanks for your love that means so much.

For my teens: Dustyn, Sydni, and Sheldyn, thanks for being good young people who strive to make your mother proud by doing the right things.

For my husband, Derrick, thanks for being my best friend who loves me so.

For my new readers, thanks for giving my work a try.

And my Heavenly Father, thanks for giving me a desire to help struggling readers find their voice and find their way so they can reach greatness.

CHAPTER 1

Caught Up

Okay, Ella, so here's the deal. You've got to help us cheat," my sassy, overbearing twin sister, Eva, said to me. Randal stood by silently, as usual. "I know you're all sweet and innocent, but we're failing US History."

I squinted, and Randal said, "Don't look like that. I know it's bad that we're asking—"

"Whatever!" Eva cut in. "She's got a ninety-eight average in US History. You and I are flunking. We don't have time to study. We can do better on the next nine weeks. We need her to carry out our plan. Shoot, it ain't like I have never helped Ella out on stuff."

I wasn't sure what my sister thought I *owed* her for, but I would be risking a lot. They were both serious. I was in a sour-pickle mess.

"I don't even know how to cheat, y'all, even if I wanted to, okay? I can help you study for it though. Eva, you're right, I know the material pretty well. It is not too late for you to get it."

My sister looked at me like what I was saying was stupid. She had already stated her case, and I was just supposed to do what she said. We were identical twins, but we certainly were opposites. She was brash and sassy. I was patient and sweet.

It was not that I had a problem bending over backwards for her. What she was asking me to do could prove fatal for both of us. If we were caught, we could be suspended, and that meant being dropped from the cheer squad we both loved.

My problem with Eva was that she did not take responsibility for the predicaments she found herself in. Okay, so we did not have the perfect home life. Our father left us when we were five. We never got any specific reason, but looking back at the pictures, my mom used to be a brick house, sort of like Eva and me. We had bodies that would make any guy's head turn. Eva liked to show hers off. I was more on the conservative side. My mom had put on some weight. I did not want to think my dad was that shallow, but looking at pictures of his new woman, who was skinnier than a stick, I could come to no other conclusion.

Eva loved playing the "poor me" card because our dad was not present in our lives. Now he had another family he called his own, and he was about to get married in a few weeks. He had a three-year-old son and another baby boy was on the way. Since she did not get the love from my dad, she gave it up to almost every guy who gave her attention. I was not calling my sister a garden tool, but if she ever got married, she certainly would be the last person wearing a white gown.

"Don't say no," Randal said. (But I was definitely going to tell them to forget it.) "Just go think about it."

There were five of us who were tighter than tight. Our crew consisted of Charli, Hallie, Randal, Eva, and me. We were all cheerleaders on the varsity football and competition squad. We would be cheering basketball too. Our main goal was to make it to state and win the title of best cheerleaders in Class 5A.

We had just come from winning a football game. We were having a sleepover at Charli Black's house so that we'd all pump each other up for our first big cheer competition the next morning. Charli was our captain and an extremely savvy cheerleader. She had the looks, the personality, the charm, and the skills. Her father was a big-time judge. We loved coming over to the Black's house because Charli had her own wing, and there were no siblings to bother us when we gathered together since she was an only child.

Charli was with Hallie in the kitchen making us snacks. As outgoing as Charli was, Hallie was even more boisterous. Ever since I had known her, she had always been so positive. She had come through a lot and was raised by her father because her mother left them when she turned into a crackhead. Charli's life was not as glamorous as we all thought, however. Her parents were trying to reconnect again. Her dad had been caught tipping out. Charli and Hallie had been hanging out together all night. They were both in love. They were both dating football players. Most ballers were jerks, but the two they had were sweetie pies.

"So what's there to think about, Ella?" my sister asked with attitude.

I said, "Well, I just can't take the test for y'all."

Eva replied coldly, "We were gonna talk about the details in a little while, but you're acting all apprehensive and stuff. One of your best friends and your sister need help."

"Smoothies and sandwiches," Hallie came in and said, holding the delicious offerings. "Come try some, Eva. Leave your sister alone. Let's eat."

"Stay out of this, Hallie. I'm talking to Ella," Eva huffed back.

"Wait, what's going on in here?" Charli said, clearly not liking Eva's tone.

"We're trying not to get kicked out of the mansion," Hallie joked.

"Settle down everybody. This is slumber party time. Ella, what's going on?" Charli asked me.

"I'm talking to her," Eva said, and she stepped in front of Charli. "That's what's going on. If you give us some space and get out of our business, we can finish."

"Eva, I'm not talking to you. I'm asking Ella," Charli responded. She seemed to be the only one out of the five of us who could stand up to my sister.

"Okay, I'll tell you," Randal cut in to avoid a standoff.

"Hush, girl," Eva snapped. Then she gave Randal a little push.

My sister's rude actions were a red flag to me. If Eva did not want to tell her plan to Hallie and Charli, then my apprehensions were right on. If it was no big deal, then what was the big deal in telling them?

"They just want me to help them with the test," I said, wanting Eva to put her claws away.

"What's the big deal in that?" Hallie said. "We all need to study. First quarter exams are here. We can help each other."

Eva and Randal were silent. I looked at my sister like, *Are you going to tell her, or do I need to?* Thinking Randal was going to step out of her shy box and take ownership of what she wanted me to do was a joke.

"Not that it's any of y'all's business," Eva finally said to them when she saw that they were not going to leave well enough alone. "Randal and I need her to help us with US History, and not just studying. Heck, it's too late to get the stuff down now. We have a little plan for her to help us. She's got the class before us. She's going to fill out two copies of her answer sheet and leave one behind for us to find when we come into class after her."

"Huh? You want her to cheat? Oh heck nah. Stupid plan. It ain't happening," Charli uttered.

"She is not your sister. You can't tell her what to do. Dang, you think you can boss everyone around," Eva said to our hostess. "She's my sister and I need her. What I don't need is y'all clouding up her mind with this guilty-conscience junk that helping me is wrong."

Eva truly thought her comments were righteous. Charli did not even look at her to cosign. Instead Charli looked at me, pulled me over to a corner, and called Hallie over to us.

Charli said, "Don't let anybody make you feel like if you don't help them do something horrible that it's your fault if they fail. You have too much to lose, and you're much too sweet of a person to fall for intimidation. Tell her, Hallie."

Hallie said, "Ella, you know your sister. She wants what she wants, but everything she wants isn't good for her. That's why we're friends. That's why we're sisters: to help keep each other in line so we won't fall for the okey doke."

The slumber party we were supposed to be having was completely shot. Hallie and Charli were balled up together, talking about their guys. Eva and Randal were cornered, hoping and praying I would go against my better judgment and help them. I was stuck in between, pretending like I was asleep so that no one would bother me. All the while, I was trying to figure out what I was going to do. What was right and what could I not forgive myself for if I did not do it?

"Get up everybody. Time to go win our first competition," Charli said Saturday morning as if all hearts and minds were clear.

We were going to a meet in Loganville, Georgia. It was about forty-five minutes away, and there were four teams scheduled to compete in the 5A-4A category. Two of the teams placed in the state competition last year. However, this was a new ball game for us Lions. We had been practicing. Everybody had their tumbling. We were focused and ready to do this.

However, everyone but Charli was dragging. I had not decided what I was going to do about the whole helping Eva and Randal cheat deal, but I knew we really needed to straighten things out since had I basically divided the room by my uncertainty. Today we were a team.

I said, "Come on, girls, Charli's right. Let's go win. Hands all in. This is going to be a great day." Reluctantly, and with bad hair, bad breath, and still some bad attitudes, all of us had our hands touching. "On three."

Charli smiled my way and said, "One … two … three."

We all shouted, "Lions!" We had to be at school at eleven. It was ten. Charli's mom was fixing us breakfast while we were tripping over each other in the bathroom because we all had to hurry. I went into the bathroom where my sister was primping. She looked at me and rolled her eyes.

"Okay, so can we just talk about all this other stuff tomorrow and be a team today so we can win? Dang, drop the attitude."

"Don't tell me what to do, Ella. Besides what's going on with me has absolutely nothing to do with school."

We had our cycles on the same day too, and they had just gone off a week ago. Though Eva was usually a pretty crappy person, she was even worse during that time of the month. Since it could not be that, I wondered what was going on with her.

Caring, I asked, "Talk to me."

"I just talked to Mom."

"She okay?"

Eva vented, "Dad set a date for his wedding. Supposedly, his fiancée, Miss Samantha, wants us to be a part of it. He had the nerve to tell Mom, 'Don't worry about having to pay for the dresses because I'm gonna take care of them.' We haven't even met the lady, and he wants us to be in his wedding. He can do whatever he wants to do, but I'm not having any part of it. He needs to pay his back child support before talking about some dresses."

Eva said one thing, but her body language was saying another. She was devastated that my dad had officially planned a date to move on with his life. It probably did not matter. He had been living with his other family for years. Just the fact that he was tying the knot made me sink down on the closed toilet and hold my stomach. I felt physically ill. Eva was dealing with her own feelings. She did not care that I was absolutely upset. She left me in the bathroom to deal with my feelings. It was not that my dad did nothing for us. He was currently paying child support and got us both prepaid phones. Without even thinking, I dialed his number. When he answered, I just held the phone.

"Hello? Eva ... Ella ... one of you girls. Is that you?"

"It's me, Daddy, Ella," I said, a little salty that he did not even lock in our numbers.

He was our father, and he was still having trouble telling us apart. I guess you needed to spend time with people to know them. Maybe that was just it. He did not want to get to know us at all. We did not spend much time talking. I told him what was up with our day. What was going on in our world, and that I would think about his offer of being in his wedding. I was just being nice. However, I sensed that he seemed moved.

When we got to the school, all twenty cheerleaders were nervous. No one was talking, smiling, or kidding around. When Coach Woods came out of the gym, she asked us to load into our cars. Though cheerleading was a sport, we did not get a bus.

"Girls, gather around," Coach Woods said.

She was the best cheerleading sponsor in the whole world. She cared about us, but she was tough on us. None of us wanted to let her down.

"I need to check you guys to make sure you have everything you need."

Eva had on the wrong shoes, and three of the girls did not bring their warm-up suits. Basically, we did not look one hundred percent uniform. Whitney, our high maintenance co-captain, was pissed.

"Shoot, I left the directions on my desk," said Coach Woods. "Ella, go on in there and grab them. The door will automatically lock behind you. Here are my keys; don't leave them."

I had never been in the school building when no one else was in there. Though it was daytime, it was dark inside. When I got to the locker room areas, I had to pass by the boys' side. I heard noise. When I went closer to the opened door, I heard water running.

Truly being a scaredy-cat, I had no idea why I went over to investigate. The sight I saw was one I'll never forget. Being a virgin, I had never seen a guy's nude frame. There stood the most gorgeous specimen I could ever imagine. It was Leo Steele, our starting defensive end who was also in our junior class. His backside was to me. I probably would have passed out had he turned around.

I wondered why he was taking a shower in the school when everyone was gone. Then I saw him hit the wall and slide down it in despair. I knew something was not right. Something also was not right with me, as I was flabbergasted at the sight of him. I must have knocked over a trash can as I exited, and I hoped he did not see me. I grabbed Coach's directions and got out of the school building as fast as I could. But I'd never forget what I had just seen.

When we got to the competition, we entered in a disorderly manner. Worse yet, other teams around us, even teams we were not competing against, were locked hand in hand or walking single file, bag on the right side, and outfits perfectly coordinated. I'm not saying we looked ghetto, but we did not look polished.

"Hey, girls," my dad said. His arrival was a surprise right before we were going on. "I brought your little brother, Evan, to meet you all. He wanted to come and see his big sisters perform."

"Who told you to be here? How did you know where to find us? Mom would not have told you," Eva grumbled. She looked over at me with accusing eyes.

I said, "I mean, I talked to him and told him we had a competition. He asked where. I didn't know he was coming."

Eva yelled, "I can't tell you anything. Why'd you call him? What did you say? You're going to be in his stupid wedding?"

"All right, Eva, settle down," my dad pleaded. People started looking over at us.

"You think I care, Dad, what these people in here think? Please, and I'm certainly not taking orders from somebody who left us." Eva walked over to Coach Woods. "Coach, isn't it time for us to go on?"

Coach Woods was caught off guard, and the rest of the team was dumbfounded. She shrugged at my father who told her it was okay. Our problem was that we were all off focus. When we performed, we dropped all five of our stunts. In the tumbling rotation, a couple of girls ran into each other. Some of us had no facial expressions and were not smiling. Overall we were not even close to tight. The girls from Loganville and Ola were exceptional. Heritage High School was just okay, but because we were so pitiful, I knew we would not place.

Whitney said, "Ugh, we just look a mess. All black squad and we have no buckets or bows; we just look bootleg. If this is how our squad is going to be, we don't need to go to another meet because we're not representing Lockwood well."

Cheerleading was supposed to be about yelling out and being proud. However, if girls had many issues in their home life, issues of security, issues of togetherness, how could they be cheerful? Maybe Whitney was right. Maybe we were in over our heads and needed to just stick to cheering on the sidelines.

I could not believe I agreed to help Randal and my sister cheat. There I was in US History, ready to forsake my morals, bracing myself to carry out Eva's plan, and scared as heck. My teacher was Mrs. Green, a frail-looking older lady who was not too hip. People would ask her permission to go to the bathroom and not come back until the period was almost over. She would inquire what took so long and any dumb answer they gave, like, "I felt sick, so I just stayed in the bathroom so I could catch my balance," Mrs. Green would buy it.

Instead of taking one Scantron sheet when she passed them out, I took two. As we began to take the test, I filled out both sheets. However, I only turned one in to Mrs. Green. We were on block classes. Therefore, we had ninety minutes per class. When everyone turned their tests in, there was still twenty-one minutes left in the class. Mrs. Green turned around and put the Scantrons through a machine.

"Well, I want to say most of you guys did not study for this exam. I had one A, one B, and the rest Ds and Fs. Congratulations to Ella. You earned a ninety-seven, so it'll only be a three-point curve."

The rest of the class booed me. Too bad they didn't study. Eva's plan was for me to leave the second Scantron under my seat and beneath my jacket. People left things in the classroom all the time, and Randal was supposed to distract Mrs. Green while Eva found the Scantron and copied down the answers. They would have time to do that because they had Mrs. Green after lunch.

The plan went awry because the two social butterflies passed the Scantron on to friends in Mrs. Green's other US History classes. The majority of Mrs. Green's students failed the test. Most people in Eva and Randal's class had the exact same score as I did. The dummies did not even take the whole class period to do the test. People turned in their papers in fifteen minutes or less. She smelled cow manure, and my legs were knee deep up in it.

I was in PE with Coach Woods when I got called up to the office. I wanted to find my sister to ask if they tore up the Scantron, but the school year was still new. I did not remember her classes or where she was at that moment. Walking to the office, I thought certainly I would be able to talk myself out of any trouble because I had never been to the principal's office before. However, I was shaking.

"What's going on, Miss Blount? I've seen your sister a whole bunch of times, but I thought you were the good one," Dr. Sapp, our fine principal, said to me. Mrs. Green stood there, rocking back and forth. "Mrs. Green came to me with some interesting, yet possibly disturbing news. She thinks you cheated on her exam."

I defended myself. "But, Mrs. Green, you watched me complete my test. I answered everything on my own."

Mrs. Greene explained, "I saw you taking your test, Ella, and I don't believe that you cheated on your *own* exam, but it's the class that came after you that I am having a tough time with. I can't figure out how they got your *exact* score."

"Maybe I wasn't the only one who studied," I said.

Not buying it, Mrs. Green said, "Your sister is in my other class, Ella. Her poor work ethic all quarter does not match up to the almost-perfect score she received. More is going on here, and I've never known you to lie."

Not knowing all Eva had done to hang me out to dry, I rationalized, "But can you explain to me what you think I did, Mrs. Green? If you gave them the same test you gave me, and we got the same score, what's the problem? You're right, Eva's my sister. We studied together, no big deal."

"The question you missed was not a hard one. For fifteen people in my class to miss the same one and get everything else correct did not seem right. So I gave them another test."

"What happened?" Dr. Sapp asked.

Mrs. Green said, "They all put down the exact same answers."

"There you go. People studied," I said.

Shaking her head, Mrs. Green said, "Problem was, Ella, I changed up the questions, and they put the exact same answers. If they studied, then they would have understood that what was question one on the first test was question six on the second test. Of course they all failed the second test, but nobody wants to tell me anything. Something's not right. When the class was gone, I looked under your desk and found this: a filled-in Scantron."

"I don't see anybody's name on it," cool Dr. Sapp answered Mrs. Green.

"That's right, but I'm just wondering if we can take it over to the forensics lab down in the technical building and see if Ella's fingerprints will show up. She turned hers in to me, so why would there be a second one with all the answers filled in under her desk? Anyone could have used it, particularly people from the next class who hadn't taken the test yet."

At that moment, I lost it. I could not say everything was okay. I could not say I had not done anything. I came clean. I said I left the Scantron there but didn't know if anyone would actually use it. I admitted that it was all my doing. Dr. Sapp told Mrs. Green that he would handle it from there.

When she stood up, she said, "You know, Ella, you've always been a lady with such integrity. It's hard for me personally right now. I wish I could retire, but with this recession we're in, I'm just not able to. I would never think kids would take advantage of me like this, particularly my better students. I am battling multiple sclerosis, barely even able to hold on, walk, much less keep my head up. Now I'm going to have to be on my guard for sure because I can't trust anybody. Thank you for showing me I should have no faith in the next generation. Another reason I can't retire any time soon is because I have to stay here and tighten up on you guys so you all won't try to get over on another soul again."

She walked out. I hung my head low. The lady did not deserve my bad actions.

"Gosh, girl, you done hurt the lady's feelings," Dr. Sapp said to me, trying to joke around.

"Sir, I'm so sorry."

"So you know you can get suspended for cheating."

"But I didn't actually cheat. I didn't know if anybody would actually copy it."

"Ugh, don't try to justify your actions," he scolded.

"But I'm a straight A student. Please, sir. I'm on the cheerleading squad. We're trying to win state, and we bombed out at our first meet. You always told us that you used to get in trouble back in the day. Can I have *one* courtesy pass?"

"Dang, my speeches get me in trouble," Dr. Sapp said. "All right, I'm going to tell you what I'm going to do. I'm going to give you ISS, in-school suspension, for five days. This way you're on the squad. I know if you get suspended from school, you're immediately off the team, and I do think you deserve another chance. However, taking the hit for anybody, your sister in particular, is unwise. I know Miss Eva, and she can be persuasive and lead you to do all kinds of stuff. You did not help her or anybody else by cheating for them."

"Yes, sir."

"Now get your self to ISS down the hall. You'll have all week to think about your actions. You'll probably be the laughing stock, and I hope you can handle it. Maybe the embarrassment will keep you from doing something this stupid again. Mr. Hatcher is out this week, so I'm actually going to be the ISS teacher. I'm going to make sure you get everything done. You might be able to sneak out on Mrs. Green, but not Dr. Sapp. I've been around the way, and I know how to make sure you pay."

"So do I get my books? Do I go to ISS tomorrow? What?"

"Weren't you listening? You head on down there right now. I already have two kids in there."

When I walked to ISS, I could not believe who was sitting in the tight space. It was Leo Steele, the guy I had seen naked. He was looking like he was about to break someone's jaw. He looked up and saw me, and he stared really hard. I wondered if he saw me the other day.

"Get to moving on in there and sit down," Dr. Sapp commanded, interrupting my thoughts. "There's no need in delaying the inevitable. You're going to be in here with me all week. Your books and assignments are on their way so you can stay caught up.

CHAPTER 2

Rescue Needed

Why are you looking at my pants?" Leo boldly asked me when Dr. Sapp gave us a break.

I shook my head and looked away quickly. I did not realize I was imagining him with his clothes off. I had never noticed Leo Steele before. I mean, he was just a big, dumb jock who always got in trouble. The football field seemed like a perfect place for him. He was a defensive end, the one who—more times than not—sacks the quarterback. He had the speed, size, and muscles to do it.

The ISS room was extremely tiny. It was barely a storage closet. Everybody knew Dr. Sapp did not play. There were hardly any people in ISS. Most of the time people were just sent home for suspensions.

I was staring at Leo's chest when I heard, "Earth to Ella. What's wrong with you?" Leo asked. "What are *you* doing in here anyway? I could see if it was Eva, but you're the good sister," Leo said, making me aware that he knew me.

Being too sweet had its disadvantages. Everyone thought I had no spunk. I was sort of sick and tired of everyone saying that. I did not want to have a reputation of being bad, but I didn't want to be seen as Little Miss Perfect either.

"Leo, you don't know me," I cautioned "You don't know what I'm capable of doing."

"Okay, dang, you got a little fire," he said, taken aback that I snapped. "But I know you can't get in trouble."

"Then you don't know her. She was the one who helped people cheat," this other dude in ISS said.

Leo and I looked at each other like, *Uh, okay, were we talking to you?* It was weird that Leo and I connected—well, maybe not that weird. Though we did not hang, our circles were the same. We were in the popular crew. We just never noticed each other. Now, I surely was noticing him.

"I'm Carlen," the other dude said, extending his hand. He took it back when he realized the two of us were uncomfortable. "I stole someone's iPod. And Miss Cheerleader is in here because she helped so many people get an A on their US History exam."

"Oh, you were the one who was supposed to leave the answers on the Scantron sheet?" Leo snorted.

"How does everybody know about that?" I asked.

Leo explained, "Your sister was selling the answers to everyone."

At that point I was furious. Eva was a trip. She asked me to help her, but she was using me more than I knew. She was a selfish witch.

Carlen looked at me and said, "And he's in here because he was fighting with the Axes."

Immediately I cringed. The Axes were the leading gang at our school. Everybody knew they did not just talk trash; they had proven they were violent.

"Like you just said, we don't know each other," Leo said to me coldly. "So don't act like you're concerned."

Thinking maybe I did not need to like him, I snapped, "Fine, but they're nothing to play with."

Dr. Sapp came into the room. "Ella, please step out in the hallway."

When I did, I immediately got grabbed by my shirt. My mom was there. She was not happy.

"Okay, Dr. Sapp, you need to turn your head because I'm not getting reported for child abuse," my mother stated.

He laughed, not knowing my mom was serious. She did not laugh. Dr. Sapp stepped back and looked the other way.

My mom stepped to me harshly. "I get a call that you're in ISS. What in the world, Ella? This is crazy. Cheating?"

I could not say anything about my sister's involvement because I did not want to incriminate her to the principal. He already handed out his punishment. I had to be in ISS the whole week. It was not going to be that big of a deal. I got to make up my work. So why did she come all the way down here to trip?

Trying to calm her down, I said, "Mom, I made a mistake. I'm sorry."

"You're darn right you made a mistake. I'm just so disappointed in you, Ella, with everything else I got going on right now. I get called at work about you being suspended."

"I'm not suspended, Mom. I'm in in-school suspension."

"Right, in-school suspension. Can you walk your butt to a regular classroom right about now? No? She has to stay locked up in here and for how long, sir?"

"Five days," Dr. Sapp said, trying to hold in his laughter.

He was a man with a doctorate, and he thought it was funny that my feisty mom came up here and showed her tail. I saw him checking her out. My mom, however, was focused on keeping me in the fire.

"If there were more mothers like you, trust me, my job would be a lot easier," he praised. He was practically flirting with my mom.

She was so high on the collar she did not get it. I knew I was going to have to look into Dr. Sapp's life. We liked him and thought he was extremely cool, but was he married? Did he have a family? Nobody knew. He was at the school twenty-four-seven. I doubt that he was married, and by the way he was looking at my mom, I thought I could leverage his emotions and ask him if I got him a date, would he let me off with a warning.

My mom peeked her head in the classroom and said, "It doesn't look like there are too many distractions. Thank you so much, Dr. Sapp."

My blushing principal uttered, "Oh no ... no problem."

He told me to get on in there and get back to work. He stayed out there grinning and chees-ing. My mom shook her head at me, so I knew I was going to get it even more later.

"Looks like someone's going to be in trouble when they get home," Carlen joked.

His mannerisms were almost too girlie, but he was kind of cool too. Carlen motioned like he was whipping me. Leo laughed.

"Right, big football player, what are you go-ing to say when your mom comes up here with her switch," I joked, but Leo seemed to close up as he looked away and hit the desk.

"Someone's on his cycle," Carlen whispered to me.

The next day I was actually looking forward to ISS. That was kind of scary because I knew I longed to see Leo. I had never been into a boy. I fixed myself up nice and made sure I looked really cute. I could not stop imagining him with his birthday suit on.

Having Dr. Sapp monitor ISS was the best because he was constantly walking the halls and doing other stuff a principal needed to do. He trusted us to get our work done. Carlen and I did. Leo kind of looked at the four walls.

"You better get on your work," I said to him.

Being a jerk, Leo said, "You better stay out of my business."

I was curious about what was going on with him. Being up here on a weekend when the place was supposed to be locked up still had me wondering. Also, when I made mention of his mom coming the day before, why did he get so angry?

When lunch was brought to us, I pried. "Where do you live?"

"Didn't you just say we needed to get our work done?" Leo asserted.

Carlen leaned in and offered the answer. "No one knows where he lives now because he and his mom just got evicted."

"You know everything," I said to Carlen. Leo looked frustrated.

I think Leo opened up to me because he was hungry and wanted my food. It was like the boy had not eaten in a couple of days. It did not take me long to realize maybe he did not have a home. I thought back to when I caught him showering in the locker room after the school was locked up. Maybe he was living here. Where was his mom? How was he going to take care of himself?

Certainly the football coach, Coach Strong, did not know he was staying on school property.

Watching Leo devour the food like an animal, I had to figure out a way to help the untamed lion who growled at everyone. I felt like that was a mask. There was something in his eyes that told me he was going through a lot. Maybe that's why I allowed myself to get into trouble—to be Leo's angel.

Dr. Sapp came back and demanded our assignments. Carlen was just happy to turn his in. Leo started to fluster.

I said, "Doc, here's mine and Leo's."

"What do you mean yours and Leo's?" Dr. Sapp asked.

"Well, we pretty much have the same classes. So we sat and did it together, you know, to save paper and make the world green and all."

"What?" Dr. Sapp squinted and turned to the know-it-all in the room. "Carlen, is this true?"

"You heard the lady, sir. I watched them talk," Carlen said, covering me.

"You didn't say we couldn't," I pleaded to Dr. Sapp.

He took the work and put it on his desk. They he went to talk to Leo.

"Your Mr. Defense could have said thanks," Carlen whispered.

"How about I say thanks to you? You really saved it," I said to my new buddy.

"I got your back, girl. Another tip, tell all your cheer friends they need to get some teeth whitener. Too many of them show yellow when they smile. Unattractive," he mused.

I caught Leo looking over at me. I could not tell if he was appreciative, but I didn't want his appreciation. That's not why I did it. He needed a hand, and whether he was grateful or not, I gave him one.

"Okay, Miss Lady, this is the second time this week that you got me playing Little Red Riding Hood," Hallie said. We were driving to the school at night in Hallie's beat-up car to take Leo a basket of food that I'd made for him.

I told my mom that one of my friends was homeless, and she made extra for dinner. I told her it was a football player, and as much as she liked sports, she considered it her contribution to the Lions, who were doing exceptionally well. I was not going to actually take the basket to Leo; he was way too prideful for that. I had Hallie park her car around a corner. I was able to peek into the coach's office, and when I saw Leo turn his back, I knocked on the window. When he turned around, there was a note taped to the glass with an arrow pointing down. I was sure he had a way to get back in the school. I got the baskets from the dollar store, so whether he was trashing them or keeping them, it did not matter because each day there was another fluorescent-colored one sitting there.

"I think I want to actually talk to him this time," I said to Hallie.

"Bad idea, Amir told me Leo is real tough."

"You haven't told Amir what is going on, have you?"

"No."

It was really weird that Hallie had a boyfriend now. Charli and Eva always had someone following them, but Randal, Hallie, and I were always on the sidelines. I was happy for my girl, and a part of me wanted to know what having a steady guy felt like. I kept worrying about Leo, wondering if he was okay, and praying nobody found out what he was doing. The last thing I wanted was for him to end up in jail. He did not even know I knew, so I could not mention it to him, but I knew we were connected.

"So you think I should not say anything?" I asked Hallie again, making sure she was giving the best advice.

"If he knows that you know, then he's going to be scared that someone else knows. If he does not have anywhere to go, and he has to leave here because he does not want to get caught … but he has nowhere to go, so where's he gonna go?" she added, absolutely confusing me. "You really like Leo Steele?"

"Well, you know about him. You guys went to the same elementary school and stuff. Should I like him? He's awfully mean. Paint him green and call him the Hulk already."

"He's actually pretty caring. His dad died in a car accident when Leo was in the third grade, so he had to repeat it because he was out so long."

"Why was he out so long?" I asked.

"He was in the car too. He had a lot of broken bones, but he survived. He's just been an angrier person ever since. He's fine though, girl." I just smiled. She patted my knee and said, "You're doing a good thing by helping him. Maybe you're the girl who can change his heart from steel to gold."

"Let's get out of here. You know if he sees your car, he's gonna think it's you helping him."

"Oh my gosh, you think?" Hallie added, not wanting anything to mess up her relationship with Amir.

"Just playing," I joked with her.

She let out a deep sigh of relief. We were ready to jet. She tried starting her car, but the engine would not turn over.

"Come *on*! My dad just fixed this thing not too long ago. I wish I could get me a brand new one like Charli," Hallie remarked.

I kept it real. "Girl, at least you riding. Don't get frustrated. Give it just a minute, and then let's try it again."

Before we could try again, three cars came racing into the school parking lot.

"That's Shameek and the Axes," Hallie called out.

"Get this car started so we can get out of here," I replied, knowing what the Axes were capable of. "If they drive around and find us, those fools might try to rape us for initiation."

"Oh my gosh! You know, you are right." Hallie's voice trembled.

We made sure the Axes were on the other side of the school. Then Hallie tried once again to get us moving. Both of our hearts sank when the car would not start.

"Just get really low," Hallie said. Then she picked up her cell phone.

"Who you calling?"

She showed it to me. It was Amir Knight. She pushed the speaker.

"Hey, babe, what's up?" he said in a sweet tone.

Hallie whispered as if the Axes could hear us. "This is gonna sound a little crazy, but I just wanted to let you know that I'm in the school parking lot with Ella."

"It's nine o'clock," Amir noted.

"I know, just hear me out. Something's going on with my car, and the Axes are up here racing each other. I just wanted to let you know if I don't call you back in ten minutes, come up here or send the police."

"They're going through initiation," he said quickly, confirming the word around the school to be true.

Hallie said, "I know. Ella just told me."

Amir asked, "Why are y'all at the school?"

I snatched the phone. Then I pressed the red button to end the call. Hallie got upset.

She yanked the cell back. "Why'd you do that?"

"You can't tell him," I said.

"Look, they're getting out," Hallie said. We saw about eleven guys get out of three cars with spray paint.

Leo must have heard the noise from inside the school because he came out, and all we could see from the car was a big commotion. Leo was going off on Shameek. Suddenly, he was surrounded by the Axes, and they were beating him up. It was horrifying to watch.

I tried to get out of the car. "Oh my gosh!" I screamed. "I gotta do something."

Hallie held my shirt and yelled, "Don't you dare!"

Something had to be done. I could not keep watching and do nothing. I picked up Hallie's phone and dialed 9-1-1.

"Hello, what is your emergency?" the operator asked.

"We're in the Lockwood High School parking lot, and a gang was drag racing and spray painting the school. Now they're beating up a kid. Send an ambulance and the police, hurry! They won't stop," I sobbed.

Hallie took the phone from me because I was shaking so badly. She called Amir back. I was so out of it. I did not know what she was saying.

I finally heard sirens. The coward gang guys got in their cars and sped off. A police car got there after the guys left. It was so dark out there. I got out of the car and made sure that the ambulance knew exactly where the patient was. I ran as fast as I could over to Leo, and when I bent down, I could see his face looked unrecognizable. My heart was breaking.

Hallie and I had to give statements to the police, but she and I both knew that we needed to be generic. We could not describe any cars. We could not describe any people, because if they found out, we'd be their next hit. Amir pulled up, and Hallie rushed to him.

"Coach Strong is going to meet us at the hospital. Leave your car and just get in my car. Your dad can get it tomorrow," Amir commanded. Then he became emotional as we saw the ambulance drive away. "I knew something was going on with Leo, dang it."

An hour later, I snuck my way back into the emergency room where Leo was behind a curtain. He was resting. I had to make sure he was breathing. Thankfully, he was.

As I turned to leave, he awoke and grabbed my hand. "You … Ella, thanks."

He tried to smile, but cringed at the pain he was feeling in his face and in his ribs. Hating that I could not have done more, a tear fell from my cheek. He reached up to wiped it away.

Leo mumbled, "I'm gonna to be okay."

"Hey," a nurse called out, startling me. "You're not supposed to be in here."

I left quickly. As I rushed out, I bumped into Coach Strong. He looked at me like I knew something, and I looked at him like I wanted to reveal all.

"Tell me what's going on," he asked.

"You gotta help Leo," I said. "I don't know why, but he has nowhere to live. He's been staying at the school. Please, don't tell him I told you, but you gotta help him, sir."

Before I could be asked more questions, I jetted away. The coach heard me, so I hoped he would fix Leo's dilemma. I could not take my heart breaking over his plight for another second.

Leaving the hospital, I was a nervous wreck. Leo and I were not in a relationship. He was not my boyfriend. I do not even think we were friends, but he had affected my world, and I wanted to protect him. I wished it was me lying there instead of him. As soon as I saw Hallie and Amir waiting on me in the parking lot, I went up to my girlfriend and hugged her tight.

"I just can't believe this, Hallie. If the police wouldn't have come, the Axes would have killed him. They need to be stopped. I'm turning in their names."

Hallie shook me hard. "Oh no you aren't! Leo knows those guys, and he can handle himself with them."

"If they're in jail, how are they going to come after me?"

"We didn't see each and every one of them. If you go after Shameek, the rest of them will come after you. Just leave it alone," my girlfriend said.

Amir reasoned, "Look, Ella, I know how you feel. I've been beating myself up out here. I've talked with Hallie for the last few minutes about wishing I'd done more. You got help, and as you said, if you hadn't who knows what would have happened. Feel good about that. I'm gonna talk to my dad about him staying with us for a while until all of this gets figured out. He can't be living at the school. Dang."

I uttered, "Well, I just saw Coach Strong, and I talked to him. Leo's gonna hate that."

"Yeah, but Coach needs to know," Amir chimed in.

"Thank you," I replied to Hallie's boyfriend. "I had to do what was right."

They drove to my apartment, and I was feeling really sad. Amir asserted, "It's gonna be okay."

I nodded as I exited the car. I was actually happy that my mom's car was not there. It was cool that I did not have a curfew. My sister was always out. This was good since I just wanted to go to sleep.

However, I walked in the apartment and saw my sister in the middle of the family-room floor dancing seductively to loud music. I heard two male voices from the couch, cheering her on. I lost it. Those were two boys from the Axes.

"Oh, now we can really have a party," one of the boys with the worst haircut I'd ever seen smirked as he came up to me.

I shouted, "Get out of my house! I'm going to call the police. I don't want you guys here!"

Eva declared, "You can't tell people what to do. This is as much my place as it is yours."

"Get out of my house!" I screamed again, ignoring Eva's demand.

I rushed over to the house phone and started dialing. I pushed number nine. I gave them a second to think it over as I held my finger right near the number one.

"Man, we ain't got time for this. We already outran the cops earlier tonight."

"Oh my gosh! Oh my gosh!" I cried, not wanting to reveal that I could identify two more guys other than Shameek who I knew were involved in Leo's beating.

Eva said, "I don't know what's wrong with my sister. We'll pick up the party another time. I only did a little show, so you don't owe me the whole twenty, but at least give me ten."

"Nah," the guy with blotchy skin said. "It was an all-or-nothing deal, baby."

Bad-hair boy came and fondled my sister's behind. "If you really want the big bucks, you know what you got to do."

"I'm not doing that, Neckbone," she protested. Then she opened up the door and they left.

I looked at her like she was a tramp. How could we be twins when her mind was so warped?

"Oh, quit looking at me like you're so goody-goody."

"Well, I'm not a slut!" I yelled out.

She came over and tried to slap me, but we were equals so neither of us won; we were just tussling all over the place.

"You make me sick!" she screamed out.

I roared back, "I've been in ISS, and you haven't even said thank you or sorry!"

She just shrugged her shoulders like she owed me nothing.

"What is *up* with you? Why you got these gangbangers in our house?" I shouted.

"Just doing a little dancing for money," Eva drawled.

"What if those two boys would've just taken it?" I questioned.

She went over to the couch and lifted up the cushion. There was a sharp kitchen knife laying right there. My sister was a nut, not a fool. There was a difference.

"I'm ready for them, okay?" Eva kept making her case.

"But two of them against you? You might not have made it over here to the couch to get the knife. And are you ready to kill somebody anyway? Like the cops would even believe that you weren't expecting to run some train. You got them in our house, Eva, use your freaking brain!"

"I did. That's why you're the one in ISS and not me," she bragged.

"Yeah, but you tricked me," I snapped.

"I did not trick you. I asked you to help me."

"You asked me to help you and Randal. You were supposed to take the Scantron, but you left it there for other people. You took money for my answers. How could you do that to me?"

"I did that for you."

"Are you on *crack*?" I screamed.

"You might have book smarts, Ella, but you don't have street smarts, okay? I mean, why do you think Mom is working all the time and still not making ends meet? We're two months behind on rent, and her car might get repossessed. She needs some help, girl, or we're gonna be on the streets. So if I gotta dance for some money ... if I gotta help people cheat to get some money … if I gotta sell out my sister to get some money, then I'm gonna do whatever I can to help my mom because that's who I am. You stay the good one. If you gotta go to ISS to cover me, then I don't feel any sympathy because some of the things I'm willing to do to help, you can't do."

I sunk down on the couch. I hadn't noticed that things had gotten so bad. My dad was over there planning some lavish wedding, and we could barely even keep a roof over our heads. It was a hot mess.

Reading my mind, Eva continued, "And that prima donna lady our dad is with should make sure he takes care of all his kids, not just hers. So though you think I got a lot of problems, I'm the last of your worries. We've got bigger problems; there's a rescue needed."

CHAPTER 3

Keep Quiet

Dad, the absolute last thing either of us wanna do is go to your house and play like all is right with the world with your new family," Eva declared. My father stood in front of us. He was trying to bond with his daughters, but my sister shot his idea down fast.

My sister was so domineering. I could not get a word in edgewise. My father's eyes said what his words would not. They were watery. They held sadness. But he couldn't make eye contact with either one of us.

Eva had my dad exactly where she wanted him, so she went for the jugular. "You chose what family you wanted to be with," she said. "Don't think we wanna be a part of it. If you want to help us, pay your back child support 'cause our mama is working all these jobs to make up for the difference you won't pay. She should take your butt to court, but she's too sweet to do that."

"Eva!" I scolded.

"No, I am okay to listen," my dad said.

Clearly, my dad was letting me know that I did not know him at all. I thought she was being very disrespectful; however, he was giving her the leeway to vent. That was admirable in my opinion. He had not done all that he should, but he was standing there wanting to change. Maybe he did not want to bring a bad omen to his new marriage. Maybe he did miss us. Maybe his wife-to-be was begging him to include us. Why did I have to figure out his reasons? As long as he was genuine, then it should not matter.

"Look, I've already talked to your mom. She said you guys can come."

"And why is my mom not here?" Eva vented. "She's not here because she's working, taking somebody else's shift."

My dad said, "Okay, Eva, I've listened to you give your thoughts. You girls are older now, and I haven't explained why I left. We need time to bond and talk. I'm not saying it was right to go, but please don't hold me completely responsible for what your mom does or doesn't do with her own life."

Eva said, "She had dreams and goals. She got pregnant and had twins. You're the one who went to school while she worked as a waitress. She told us."

"Your mom also knew we were not ready to have children. You girls are a blessing and … you know what? Forget it," my dad said, watching his words.

"Wait, what you trying to say? That Mom trapped you?" Eva scoffed.

"You weren't there," I finally spoke up.

She questioned, "What, you're on his side? You believe him? We were a mistake?"

"They were eighteen. He was in college, and our mom was a local in the town. We were not planned. Come on, Eva."

"Then he should not have done the tangle if he did not want to risk getting caught up, Ella."

"Yeah, well, one was wearing a condom and the other manipulated the rubber because she was ready to get out of her mom's house," my dad retorted. Then he turned and walked to the door. "I should not have said that. Forget it. Sorry I came here."

"You should be sorry now, trying to say this whole thing was our mom's fault," Eva ranted.

I rushed the door and stood in front of it. "Dad, don't go. It's a work day at school. We don't have to go in tomorrow. I want to spend the night at your house. I want my dad in my life. Eva doesn't speak for me."

"Well, as stupid as you are sounding, I should be speaking for you," Eva raged. "But go on, go ahead. You'll learn the hard way. Like he really, really cares for us. Seriously, c'mon."

My dad saw I was serious and said, "Great, I'll wait out in the car. Thanks."

As soon as my dad stepped outside, my sister got in my face. I tried to walk around her to pack, but she stood her ground. Usually she ran me. Not this time though.

"Please," I told her, "let's just agree to disagree on this one."

Eva said, "I don't understand you. Why do you even want to hang out with him?"

Caring what she thought, I said, "I've always admired how Hallie is close to her dad. I know Dad left long ago, but I miss his strong arms around me. I want to be told I'm beautiful by the one man who should love me the most. If I got an opportunity to have that, regardless of how I got here ... regardless of his past decisions ... regardless of what my twin sister thinks, then I'm going to go for it."

"You too doggone sweet," Eva lamented. Then she stormed to my mom's bedroom and slammed the door.

Quickly, I picked up the phone and dialed my mom. "Hey, I know you're working."

"Yeah, baby, but what's up? I just got a second."

"Mom, I just wanted to make sure it was okay with you if I went to Dad's?"

"Yes, he called and told me he wanted to have you and your sister over. Is he bringing y'all back tomorrow or should I?"

"No, he's going to bring *me* back tomorrow. Eva is not going."

"That doesn't surprise me," my mother sighed. "And you're okay to go on your own?"

"Mom! We're not joined at the hip. I don't know this lady he's getting married to, but I do want to spend time with them."

"I just want you to know that if you need me for anything, call."

Soon enough I found myself in Alpharetta, Georgia. It was one of the richest parts of the metro Atlanta area. My dad had really done well for himself. Part of me wondered if I even had accurate information that my dad still owed my mom child support. With everything he had, he did not look like a man who wouldn't pay his bills.

His house was more spectacular than anything I had seen. A very pretty lady arrived at the door to greet us. She reminded me of Hallie's bubbly personality. If she wasn't eight months pregnant, I'd say she was a size 2 or smaller and definitely the opposite of my mom's size 20. My dad introduced her as Samantha.

"Sister!" a little boy I remembered seeing at the cheer competition shouted. He rushed up to me and put his arms around my legs.

"Hey, Evan," I said, swooping him up in my arms and spinning him around.

Samantha said, "Eva, please come in. Let's get you settled. I want you to know—"

"Excuse me ... um, Ella," I said, cutting her off.

"I'm sorry, Ella. It's hard to tell the two of you apart," Samantha stated.

I wanted to say, "No, it's not. We have completely different styles. Hers is more out there. Mine is more laid back. Clearly, I did not come to your house with everything in the world hanging out. I never have my body exposed, so you should know from my father's descriptions that I am Ella. Why don't you know that?" But I said nothing.

"Calvin, I'll take her up to her room," Samantha said. I followed her up the back set of stairs. "Ella, I wanted to tell you that I'm not the reason why you and your dad haven't been connecting. I think he should have a relationship with you all, but I didn't want to be the one to push it. I tried that early on in our dating relationship, and he seemed to resent me for it. In his own time I knew he would want to hang out with you all."

I didn't know where this lady was coming from. I had no clue why she was telling me this. Was I supposed to be upset that my dad did not want to hang out with me? Was she trying to get herself off the hook so I would not be against her, thinking that she was the one blocking the relationship? Either way, both of those comments seemed a little negative to me, and I thought I was here to start off on the right foot. So I just looked at her and did not respond.

"Well, you see this is the down comforter," Samantha said, pointing at the fancy plush covers. "I don't know how you do things at your house, but I'm pretty particular with our things. I would like you not to sleep on this. Please pull it off like this."

Samantha started folding it back. I actually did not know about down comforters and the finer things in life. My dad's extra money was going to her and not to my household whether it was by his choice or her demands. Clearly, Eva and I were getting the short end of the stick.

I had passed by Evan's room coming up to the guest room. His room was immaculate and four times the size of the one Eva and I shared at our apartment. He was only three and had his own bathroom!

Another baby boy was on the way, and the new baby's room looked like it was straight out of a decorating magazine. Even the guest room made me uncomfortable because it was so nice. So I just stood there after Samantha left. I did not want to mess up anything. I certainly did not know how to work the three remotes in front of me to turn on the TV.

My dad came by, knocked on the door, and said, "Come on, let's go see the rest of the house. I'm taking the day off tomorrow to hang out with you if that's okay." I smiled. "Ella, I would like us to have a chance. If you give me an opportunity, you won't regret it."

After he took me around the house for a full tour, I started to feel good about being there. I was not sure if his wife-to-be was excited I was there. However, like Eva, her feelings were irrelevant. I kept my thoughts about her to myself. I enjoyed the bathroom, the lavish bed, and the fact that I was under the same roof with my father. What a dream come true.

The day started bright and early with my father. It was like he was trying to make up for the ten years he was gone from my life all in one day. We went to breakfast. We went shopping. We went to the matinee. We went to lunch. We went by his office. My dad was a sports agent. He had his own firm. He helped great college players get selected by an NFL or NBA team. After the office tour, we went bowling. Lastly, we went to dinner. He told me to order whatever I wanted. The steak was the best I had ever had.

Over dessert, he said, "Ella, I'm really impressed with the type of lady you are. You are so kind, and you have such a big heart. Is there something you want to talk to me about?"

The rational side of me was like, "You know what, Ella, don't even go into anything heavy. Just enjoy your dad. The day has been absolutely amazing—better than any time at an amusement park could be. Keep quiet." But the heart in me, wanting our time to be genuine, demanded I get deep.

So I said, "Dad, what now? I mean, I haven't spent time with you since I was little, just off and on, here and there, but really being with you and spending a whole day with you … You have another family now, why do you care?"

He paused from eating his cheesecake and then said, "I buried my mom a few months ago."

"Ah, Dad. I'm sorry."

"It's okay. She and I weren't that close either. I got to spend some time with her before she passed. She said she regretted not really getting to know me or her granddaughters. I had to examine myself and think what I was missing out on by not being a dad. Sure, I was too young when I found out you were coming, but as your sister so eloquently said, it took two. I was man enough to try and get me a lil' somethin' somethin'. Ella, I was so bitter and angry. I felt your mom trapped me, and I never allowed myself to look at the blessing in all of it."

Hearing my dad express his heart and desire to now be in my life meant the world to me. He deeply wanted to be my father. I could have jumped up and shouted and hugged his neck so tight. However, the restaurant was very upscale, and I did not want to be ghetto.

"Nobody is promised tomorrow. We need to make the most of every day," he continued. "I tried to tell my mom it wasn't her fault. I could have reached out to her too. You and your sister are still in high school. Heck, I'm in my thirties. She said she was the parent and had made some life choices that didn't always put me first. Her talk changed me. She challenged me to get to know you girls. Actually, that was her dying wish. I might not be able to make things right with Eva, but I'm gonna try. If she doesn't let me in, it's certainly understandable. However, that will be her choice. If I can get to know one of my girls, I am much richer than if one of my players signed in the first round."

"Don't worry about Eva, Dad. She just might come around if you give her some time."

My dad said, "I don't blame Eva for her bitterness. It's my fault. But, Ella, being your dad, connecting with you this way, talking to you, apologizing, establishing a real relationship ... is priceless."

We hugged. The only thing I did not like about my time with my dad was the fact that his fiancée kept texting him every hour. It was like she thought he was out with another lady or something. Goodness gracious already, it was *my* time with *my* dad. Why was she so insecure? She did not have to trip. He did not want me to know he was annoyed, but it was pretty easy to see his frustration with her.

"We must do this again soon," he said, dropping me off back home. "If you need me for anything, please call." I hesitated getting out of the car and he asked, "What's going on, Ella? Talk to me."

"Dad, I just need you to pay your back child support. You are doing really well. You live in that big three-story house. We are in this apartment, and we are about to get evicted. You say you love me and Eva and want to have a relationship with us, but right now we just need for you to take care of our basic needs."

"Okay, I'm confused. I let it slide when Eva said it, but let me be clear, I don't owe any back child support. I'm not trying to start anything between you and your mom, and I don't like to always be the bad guy. Is this the reason why Eva hates me so? You both need to know the truth. Your mom had a boyfriend who damaged her credit. He spent all of the money I would give your mom for your support. I even had a college fund set up, and she let the joker blow it. He's gone now, but so is the money."

"You mean Trevon?"

"I don't know his name. The guy who lived with y'all for three years."

Livid, I said, "Yup, Trevon."

"I'm not in a position to dig your mom out of the hole she got herself in. I shouldn't have spent my money on some of the things I did, but I have a job and pay my bills. I live up to my responsibilities. I don't want you all to get evicted, so I will see what I can do, but I can't pay two notes. Consider coming to live with me, Ella."

"Dad, I could never," I gasped. I had heard enough.

When I got out of the car, he got out too. "Dad, I'm cool. Thanks, you don't need to help me with my bag. It's just a duffel."

He was on a mission. He walked past me and knocked on the door.

"Thanks for bringing her home," my mom opened the door and said to him.

"Erika, we need to talk right now," my dad demanded.

"Dad, what are you doing?" I said, knowing that he was going to talk to my mom about what we just talked about. Obviously, she didn't want me to know about her irresponsibility.

"I think I'll fight the courts for the girls," he said to my mom.

"What?" she shrieked.

"You are about to get evicted from your place. I should have done this when you lost their college fund. You let that loser ruin your credit, and now you are struggling to care for my girls."

"Why now, Calvin?" my mom glared at me and asked. "What have you been telling him?"

"I just asked him to pay his back child support," I whispered.

"I did not need you to do that. I did not ask you to do that. I have been working two and three jobs. Your dad doesn't need to be all up in my business."

"He does need to pay his back child support," Eva said, strutting into the family room.

"Don't go there!" I looked over and said to my sister. "You don't know everything, Eva."

"See, that's the problem I have with you," my dad said to my mom. "You got my girls thinking

that I'm not paying my bills, but you are not telling them the truth."

"There's no other truth to tell," Eva interjected again. "You owe money and have not been
paying it."

My dad defended, "No, your mom's boyfriend used it up. Smoked it up. Drugged it up.
Gambled it up. It's gone!"

"Huh?" Eva fumed.

My dad continued, "Eva, I'm not saying I'm
a perfect dad, but I do care about you. I'm trying
to make amends."

"So what? I don't want to be close to you. Too
little, too late!" my sister yelled.

Eva grabbed her jacket and exited like she
usually did when she couldn't stand the heat. I
had to stick around to put out the fire as my mom
and dad went at it. Unfortunately, neither of them
heard a word because they were both going off.

Finally, my dad left. My mom looked at me
like I had betrayed her. She went in her room
and slammed the door. I sunk to the couch, holding in all my emotions and wondering what I had
done wrong. My dad hated my mom. My mom

hated my dad. My sister hated both of them, and I could not fix any of it. What a mess!

Thankfully, this was the last day of ISS. I was starting to get a little creeped out. Having feelings for Leo Steele was bothering me. Instead of talking to him, I kept my distance.

Dr. Sapp said, "There were three of you guys in ISS, and now it's only you two. Listen, I'm going out to the halls as classes change. I expect you to keep it as quiet as it is right now. Steele, you know I'm not playing. You know I've given you a pass for staying at my school. I have no tolerance."

"Gotcha, Dr. Sapp," Leo said, looking away from me.

I had not seen him since he held my hand and told me thanks in the hospital. I wasn't sure if he knew I was the one who left him the baskets of food. Some part of me was a little bummed out that he wasn't making conversation. That's why I knew it was best for me to just get over whatever feelings I had brewing for him deep inside my soul.

Then I felt two strong arms come over my back. Then he massaged my shoulders. His husky voice whispered in my ear.

He said, "A brother gets out of the hospital, and the one who saves his life acts like she doesn't care anymore. What's up? You used to glance over here and bat your eyelashes. Now you are not even looking my way. Did I offend you?"

I quickly turned around and faced him. I was extremely uncomfortable as my heart started racing. However, I stared at him.

"You knew it was me?" I asked.

"I knew what was you? You bringing me the baskets of food or you calling the police when I was getting my head bashed in? I knew it was you for all of it."

"And you're not mad?" I asked, not able to keep a straight thought.

He took one of my hands and said, "Listen, I've never had a girl care the way you have. I do owe you an apology for giving you such a hard time in here. You helped me turn in my work. You let me eat up all of your food. And then somehow you figured out my situation."

"Why didn't you say something?"

"I don't know. I guess I have been embarrassed. Who wants to tell anyone that they were living in a school? But I figured you knew because you kept prying and asking all them doggone questions. I could not get too mad because the fried chicken, them collard greens, and the candied yams with marshmallows and raisins were to die for. I just could not cut all that off. Tell me, how do you know how to throw down like that?"

"Nah, that was all my mom. She is awesome. Your eye still looks pretty bad," I sighed. There were cuts and bruises all over his face.

"Yeah, the Axes are crazy. Hey, I'm gonna work at the little camp on Saturday."

"What camp?" I asked.

"We got a clinic we are doing for little boys eight and under. Some kids are coming from the Boys & Girls Club, and other kids from the community to meet us and run through some practice drills. I have to do this community service because of the way I was mooching off the school. I'm the first one who needs to be there to give back. Thanks for helping me."

"You were a guy in need. It surely could have been me," I said, knowing money was tight at the Blount house.

Whacking his hand in the air not believing, he said, "Whatever."

"No, I am totally serious. We've got problems. My mama has *mad* drama. Behind on the rent and everything else."

"It ain't like she gonna leave you though," Leo said as if I could read between his lines.

I didn't know exactly what he was alluding to. I figured if he wanted to talk about it, he would. I did like the closeness we shared. He surprised me when he put his hands behind my neck and brought his lips really close to mine.

I could scarcely breathe when Leo said, "I really do thank you."

"Steele, why are you up?" Dr. Sapp barked, startling us both. "Nothing's going on here that I need to know about, is there?" he said. He brought his large body between the two of us. "You go back over there. And you, Miss Blount, sit down right here." He pointed to two opposite locations in the tiny room.

I could not help but blush Leo's way. I saw him smile back. I wondered if there was something there.

Later at cheerleading practice, things weren't so promising. Everyone had attitudes. Guess we just felt the hard work wasn't paying off.

Whitney, our co-captain and senior who was completely snobbish, stood in front of us all and whined, "You guys really embarrassed me at the first meet. If that's the way it's going to be, I don't want to have any part in this competition cheerleading squad."

"Whatever," my sister Eva sneered.

She and I had not spoken since the night before. Our crew knew there was tension between us because she was in one place while I was in the other. Randal was sitting beside her. Hallie was beside me. Charli was up front with Whitney.

"Those other squads looked at us like we were trash, like they didn't even think we should have been in the building," Eva said.

"Yeah, Eva's right," Randal agreed. "They rolled their eyes at us and looked down on us."

"And you guys are completely intimidated," Whitney called out.

"We do need to clean up our act a little bit," Charli said. "We should all wear our hair the same way."

"Uh, news flash," Eva said, "we don't all have long hair that we can throw up in a ponytail. All black hair is not the same, and extensions are expensive."

"You wear extensions for anything else you want to," I said. I was so sick and tired of her negative behind.

Eva shouted, "Like I was even talking to you!"

"This is a group meeting," I yelled back.

She got up. I got up. We were ready to throw down.

Coach Woods came out of her office and said, "Enough about what happened at our last competition. There's no use griping about it. The only reason we should focus on it is if we want to learn from our mistakes. Take some of the things and get better."

I sat. Eva sat. We had issues, but the team came first.

Coach continued, "Charli's mom is willing to do the bows. Whitney's mom is going to make the buckets, and Randal's mom is going to put some goodies in there for you guys to snack on every time."

I hated that my mom could not contribute. Financially, we were strapped. However, it was going to be nice to finish a competition and be able to go and see our names on some cute objects that held Gatorade, some snacks, and a nice trinket.

"Whatever. I don't think you gotta do what other people do," Eva said, having the worst attitude, as usual.

"Well, when in Rome, do as the Romans do," Coach Woods said. "I like my squad to be well represented. We are not second class. Now that we know there is an area for goody bags, we will comply. That's how we roll. We can show them we are worthy of first place. We have got a great routine, girls. We can win state. You've got to want it."

We all sat around pondering her challenge. I wished my sister would be more of a team player. However, I knew what drama we had at home. It was hard to smile when you were broke.

On Saturday I was back at school. I went to the football field to volunteer to pass out water to the little kids at camp. Surprisingly, my dad was there with the player he represented who was in the NFL. The starting wide receiver for the Seattle Seahawks, Royal Jackson, was an alumnus of Lockwood High School.

My brother wanted to try and play, but some of the boys were teasing him. Leo didn't know I was watching him. My dad didn't know I knew Leo. I could not believe how gentle the giant was with Evan. Before camp was over, my little brother knew how to hold the ball, tuck it away, and run for a touchdown. When they played the scrimmage football game for three- and four-year-olds, Evan scored twice. Of course my dad was overjoyed. When he thanked Leo, I went up to the two of them.

"Hey," Leo said in an excited tone.

"Hey," my dad said, happy to see me as well.

"Hey, sister," Evan said, running to my arms.

"Hey, Evan." I twirled him around like usual.

"This is your dad?" Leo asked.

"Yes," I said to him before introducing him to my dad. "This is my friend Leo."

"Wow, what a wonderful young man. You definitely got the height, weight, and size for D1. I gotta keep an eye on you. You need to keep me in mind as an agent one day, guy," my dad teased. "Leo, you know my daughter, huh?"

"Yes, sir, I didn't realize Ella was your daughter."

"Different last names, long story," I said to Leo.

"Sir, I just really want to tell you that your daughter saved me by—"

"Ugh," I pulled on Leo's shirt and gave him a look like, *Please, you don't need to tell everything. Some things we need to keep quiet.*

CHAPTER 4
Oh No

Girls, we got a problem at this upcoming competition," Coach Woods said to all of us at practice the next day.

Though we had our second big competition coming up, none of us wanted to be at the school on a Sunday. But when Coach sent out a message saying we needed to have an important meeting, we were all there on pins and needles wondering what was going on. Coach told us to stretch while she talked to Eva and Randal in her office. Now she was in front of us not looking happy at all.

"Competition cheerleading, just as with any sport, has academic responsibilities attached to it. The Georgia High School Sports Association has regulations that state you must have a two-point-*o* to compete in any sport. Two of our girls have fallen behind in this area and will not be able to compete. Thus we are going to have to adjust midstream."

"Adjust midstream? Huh? Can't we just pull out?" Hallie asked.

Coach Woods said, "No, you have ten days before the event to pull out. We are under that time period. So we're locked in. If we forfeit now, we may forfeit state. Randal and Eva are both bases, so back spots will have to step it up when it comes to stunting. We might have to change some places around in the dance so that we don't have holes, and on the tumbling passes ..."

Randal was waving her hand and Coach acknowledged her. "Yes, Randal?"

"You don't even need to say anything," Whitney interrupted. "Because you can't keep your grades up is why we're in this situation. The only thing you need to be saying is that you're sorry to all of us."

"I am sorry," Randal said sarcastically, "but I was just gonna remind Coach that I'm not a base, I'm a flyer."

"Oh my gosh, that's right, Randal. Now who's going to go up high? Ella, you can do it," Coach suggested.

In my mind I thought, "Oh no! Oh my gosh! Uh-uh." It was not that I was scared to be in the air, but although I was flexible, when I did the heel stretch I could tell I needed a little work.

"And, Whitney, we don't owe you any type of apology!" Eva shouted.

Whitney jabbed back, "Says the girl who's failing."

"Who says I'm failing? I can have a D and still not have a two-point-*o*, you idiot," Eva said.

"Okay, let's watch the name calling," Coach said.

"And we can certainly see why she's not an academic all-star. If something doesn't go Eva's way, all she wants to do is embarrass you by calling you names. Good for her," Whitney said.

"You're so sarcastic. You might as well say what you mean and shoot direct versus sliding undercover comments, which cut just as deep." Eva rolled her eyes.

Coach said, "Girls, didn't I tell you to settle down? We've got work to do."

"Can I call my mom for her to come pick me up?" Eva said.

"Honey, you aren't going anywhere. You are going to stay here and help us figure out this new formation. Besides, two weeks from now we have another competition, so you and Randal need to be here since we must practice for that as well," Coach said, making sense.

"Learning two formations is gonna get so confusing," Hallie said.

"We can do this, everybody," Charli affirmed.

The week flew by like a Learjet. It was pretty uneventful. I was speaking to no one at my house. Leo and I decided to become lab partners in chemistry, so on even days when we had that class, I looked forward to seeing him. Practices were exhausting because we tried to make the routine that looked fabulous for twenty people look dynamic with just eighteen.

Game four was humdrum. It was an away game, and we played the sorriest team in our region. Seriously, *I* could have gone out there and sacked the slow quarterback who was practically my little brother's size. We won, 56–0. On the bus on the way home, some of the cheerleaders were sitting with football players. I sat down, thinking that Eva was going to sit beside me, but she looked at me, rolled her eyes, and kept on walking to the back.

When Leo came on the bus, I started biting my lip. That was when I realized I wanted him to sit beside me, but he did not even look my way. When he got to my seat, he walked past it. I leaned my head against the window, yawned, and knew I needed to get some rest because we had a big competition in the morning. No need to stress over something that was not on anyway.

Then I heard his deep voice say, "No one's sitting by you? I'd like to if that's all right. I'll bet my shoulder would feel much more comfortable than that window."

I picked up my pom-poms and motioned for him to sit. His shoulders did feel good, better than any pillow I could remember. The sweet words he whispered in my ear made my pulse race.

"You are beautiful. Go to sleep," Leo said, and I did.

At the next cheerleading competition, we were intimidated as soon as we walked into the place. It was at a school in Suwannee, Georgia, that was two times the size of ours. There were people everywhere. We knew we were going up against eleven schools. The other teams' moms, siblings, and friends were wearing T-shirts that supported their school. They held signs to pump up their cheerleaders as well.

I think the last time we came to a meet we were too nervous to be aware of this. The only parents we had with us were Charli's mom and Whitney's mom. Other parents were working. Some of the other squads appeared to have football players in the audience cheering for them too. Our boys would probably laugh if we told them to come and support us. When we warmed up, we received all kinds of looks.

Though Eva and Randal could not perform, Coach still made them come. Maybe we should have left Eva at home because she wanted to go over to the squad that we knew was dynamic and go off. They were from John's Creek and they had a medieval theme to their outfits and routine. Every girl on that squad had two back handsprings and a standing tuck in their routine. They had twenty-four girls and did six stunts in the air, which they held for five seconds each and never bobbled.

At least we had snacks on our table that said Lockwood Lions. At the last competition it was bare, and every other team had their table filled with goody bags. We were trying to keep up, but we still looked out of place.

"Okay, I'm 'bout to go over there and tell them to quit looking at us like we're slaves. They act like they never seen an all-black squad. Goodness," Eva said with a roll of her neck at the JC girls.

I stood up and got in Eva's way. "You're not going over there. You don't even know those girls. Who cares what they think about us. You need to be helping us concentrate so we don't go out there and get embarrassed—"

Eva snapped, "Oh, y'all are gonna get embarrassed. Y'all have been dropping stunts all week. What makes you think you can go out there and hit stuff you couldn't hit before? How you practice is how you will perform … that's what Coach Woods always taught us. I don't even know why you're doing it."

"You're so negative, Eva," Hallie cried.

"I wasn't talking to you. I was talking to my sister."

"Well, quit being so negative," I retorted.

Eva shoved me. "Get out of my way."

I shoved her back. She pulled my hair. I pulled hers. The broiling altercation had been in the works for a while. The problem was we were in the holding room with three other squads, and we looked like barbarians. Whatever the teams thought of us, the reality we were showing them was worse.

"Eva and Ella, you all need to stop," Whitney yelled.

We kept tussling. However, when one of the girls from John's Creek yelled out, "I knew they were animals!" Eva and I froze, realizing we had crossed the line. We were raised better than this, and now our squad could possibly be disqualified because of our actions. It was not good.

"Daddy, can you please just come and pick me up?" I cried when I got home from the competition where we were humiliated.

"Just calm down, Ella. I can't understand what you're saying."

"You told me I could always call you and let you know if I needed something. Well, I don't wanna stay here with Mom and Eva anymore. I want to move in with you, Dad. So can you please come and get me?"

I did not like that he hesitated on the phone for a second. Did that mean he wanted to say no but did not know how to break my heart? Did that mean he had to run it by Samantha, but he did not want me to wait? Did that mean he had to talk to my mom to make sure it was okay, but he was still so mad at her that he did not care what she thought? I did not know, but I needed him to make a decision. Actually, I needed him to change my life.

"I'm going to come and get you for now, but later we'll have to—"

"Thanks, Daddy, thanks!" I cried.

"I'll be leaving in five. Don't think this is permanent; there are a lot of people to consider. This isn't just a decision you and I can make."

"Dad, I'm unhappy. You are my father. I haven't lived with you for years, and you just came in here telling Mom you wanted us. Either you want me there or you don't."

"Like I said, I'm on my way, but you have to understand that this is not permanent. If you can't get that, then I don't need to come."

"Okay, okay, just come," I said, treating my dad like he was my peer.

"Watch your tone, Ella. I don't know what's going on over there, but I can clearly tell that you are upset. However, there are rules that you are going to have to abide by here."

"It's not like I won't be respectful to your precious Samantha," I sneered.

"Ella!" my dad thundered.

A couple of hours later, I was at my dad's place. I was in heaven in my own room with my own adjoining bath and my own TV. Peace and quiet abounded. Everyone thought having a twin was wonderful, but it really was too much. We had to share everything.

I went downstairs to see what was in the kitchen for me to snack on. I did not get to walk all the way in. I heard my dad and Samantha arguing.

"Look, you could've asked me if it was okay for her to come. We're in the middle of planning this big wedding. I needed that guest room to put a lot of the wedding things in. You should have seen the way she strolled in here. She was quite comfortable," Samantha ranted.

My dad tried to calm her and said, "It's not permanent. I told her that. I haven't been able to talk to her mom about it. I haven't been able to talk to you about it."

"So you just took the kid from her apartment? We're both attorneys, Calvin. That's really crazy. Her mom has custody of her. What if she comes looking for her and calls the cops? And I don't want Evan to get all attached and then she has to leave."

"What's wrong with him getting attached to his sister?" my dad defended.

Samantha just rolled her eyes. I had a suspicion that she wasn't feeling me. Now that was confirmed. She never pushed my dad to get to know me because she wanted to be his only woman.

"You want me to go tell my daughter right now that you don't want her to be here?"

"You should've asked me in the first place before you just brought her here."

"Do you want me to tell her to leave?"

Samantha huffed and puffed and just turned away. I did not want to leave. I had to break the tension.

Stepping into the kitchen, I said, "Excuse me. Dad, do you mind taking me to the library? They are doing some tutoring up there, and I signed up to help. I was gonna blow it off, but I think it's best to get out of here."

My dad looked at Samantha, clearly upset because he knew I heard everything. He looked at her like, *See? Look what you are doing to my daughter.* She looked back at me like it was all my fault. He was my dad and even if she became his wife, as long as he wanted me in his life, I was going to be there. I was not leaving because she was making things uncomfortable. Samantha rolled her eyes at me and walked away.

"I got a couple of errands to run anyway. I'll just drop you off at the library. The one at the school?" he asked.

"Yes, sir."

"And I'll be back to pick you up. You okay with all of that?"

Worried he was flustered, I said, "As long as you're good, I'm good."

He put his arms around me. "Don't you worry about all this."

When we got to the library, he told me he was going to be back in an hour. I rushed in and just fell apart. I was putting tension on my parents. Was I being selfish by just leaving and not telling my mom? Now I had made my dad's life tougher by being some place that his future wife did not want me to be. Even all that hard work with cheerleading seemed for naught, as the parents of our competition laughed at us when our stunts failed. By the end of our routine, things were so bad the crowd was actually cheering for us to make it through the dance. It was an amazing crowd transformation that was appreciated, but it also humiliated us all. Some girls threatened to quit. Now, standing here alone in the library, it all became too much. I walked to a back corner, slid to the floor and cried.

"Ella? Are you okay?" Leo whispered, caressing my face. "I saw you rush in here, and I don't want you to be sad. You wanna talk about it?"

In a pitiful tone, I said, "What's there to talk about? I hate my twin sister. My mom hates me. I should hate her because she spent all my dad's child support and made me think he never paid it. We might get kicked out of our apartment. The cheerleaders suck. I want to live with my dad, but his fiancée hates the idea. Nothing's going right in my life."

Leo leaned down beside me and put his lips to mine. It was as if our tongues were doing a dance. Though it was new to me, nothing was forced. I took my hands and pulled him closer. We were practically on the floor already and when I leaned all the way down, he was on top of me.

He said, "I've been thinking about you. I want you. Is that okay? Can I make you feel good?"

He parted my legs. He ran his hand from the inside of my foot all the way to my kneecap. I had to move his hand before it rose any higher. Even though I had on jeans, I was getting too excited. Quickly, I sat up, got to my feet, and backed away.

"I'm sorry," he said, realizing he took things way too far.

"I have never been with a boy, that's all." I looked away.

He took his hand, placed it under my chin, and pulled it toward his face. "Don't turn away."

I said, "Leo, I care about you, but I've been too reserved to admit it. I just don't want to be with someone who doesn't feel the same way. I'm not trying to put pressure on you to say what you think I want to hear. I've got too much going on in my life right now to give it up to somebody who doesn't care."

He reached down and grabbed me. My legs automatically wrapped around his waist. He leaned me against the stacks, and we were looking eye to eye.

He boldly said, "I already told you, you have been in my thoughts. I think you know me well enough now to know that I don't have time to bullcrap anybody. If I said I like you, I really mean it. I want you to be my girl."

At that point I kissed him. His hands were roaming all over my back and even lower. It felt better than I could find words for.

Dr. Sapp caught us and said, "Ella Blount and Leo Steele, I knew y'all had something going on. And you *just* got your tails out of ISS."

Leo dropped me so hard that I almost fell down. As we stood and looked at Dr. Sapp, I felt that our guilt was obvious. We were sweating. I felt that my undergarment was not dry. And it wasn't because I'd peed my pants. Leo's jeans looked extra snug. I realized that Leo made me feel something new, and those feelings were so overwhelming.

I was so happy that Dr. Sapp only gave us a lecture. The last thing Leo and I needed was any more trouble. When I went outside to get picked up, I frowned when I saw Samantha pulling up.

Leo snuck behind me and said, "Dang, I didn't know your mama rolled like that."

"That's not my mom. That's my wicked, almost stepmother. They roll. We crawl."

He laughed and said good-bye. Samantha waved at me like all was right with the world. I desperately wanted to get in the back and play with Evan, but she had his car seat on one side and the empty car seat for the baby on the other. Even though the baby was not born, Samantha was prepared. I did like that about her, and I was trying hard not to hate on the fact that my dad's little children were going to have everything when my sister and I have struggled for years. I had barely spoken to Samantha before she was dogging me. Now that I knew where I stood with her, there was no need for us to be fake. So I stared out the window.

"Okay, I owe you an apology," she said, shocking me.

I turned to look at her, but I was not going to say, "Yeah you do," or "Okay, speak." No, if she wanted to say something else that was on her mind, then that was on her. I was not going to make her job any easier. She was dead wrong.

"You gotta understand this is just a hectic time in my life right now. I know you overheard me and your dad talking, but I'm getting ready to have this baby, and I'm planning a wedding too. I'm running after a toddler, and I still work. I'd just like to start over with you on a clean slate. Please chalk it up to my crazy hormones and not the fact that I want to have drama with my husband's daughter."

My dad was not her husband yet. I knew the only reason why she was apologizing was because she pissed off my dad. Now she wanted me to be nice.

"Whatever," I said, sounding more like Eva.

How much did one person have to put up with? Actions spoke louder than words. I hope she did not think that I was going to take her little apology at face value.

"So to prove that I really care," she said, "I'd like for you to be in my wedding. I know your dad asked you guys, and your sister said no. You're staying with us, though. Evan adores you. I know it would make your father happy to at least have one of his girls there. So I thought we could go to the mall, look at a couple of dresses … You can choose as long as it's not too provocative. I don't want your dad having a fit. Plus I want to pick up a couple of baby items. We can get something to eat and just bond if that's okay."

Earlier, my dad had given me a couple of dollars. To be able to go into my favorite stores and grab a cute outfit for school so I'd look nice for Leo was on the top of my mind. Certainly, I did want to try to see if this thing with Samantha could work out, if only for my father's sake. So I agreed to go.

When we got to the mall, the first person we saw was Eva. She was flirting with two guys. She basically thought it was cool to have their hands all over her. It was a public place, and she was just inappropriate.

"Is that your twin? Is that Eva? Oh my. I am so glad *that* girl is not the one at my house; she is way too mature. Can't wait to tell your dad about her," Samantha said.

Though I was so mad at Eva, I did not want Samantha to talk about her like that. Samantha was saying the same things I was thinking; however, it was not her place to say them. My sister was so into her world she did not even notice us. I did not respond to Samantha talking about Eva, and she finally got the point that I was not cool with her innuendos.

Going to the dress shop was a whole separate dilemma. Every dress Samantha liked, I thought was hideous. Every dress that I wanted to wear, she thought was too skimpy. It wasn't that she didn't want me to look cute, we just had different tastes. Finally, we found a dress we both liked.

"Toys, Mommy, toys," Evan begged.

"Ella, I need to go to the restroom. This baby is pressing down on my bladder. Could you please take Evan over to the toy store across the way? I'll be right over there. Then we can eat and go."

"Sure, no problem," I said, knowing that the only thing I wanted to do was buy me an outfit and then dip into the Body Shop.

Before I could browse, my sister came out of the dressing room. "Look at you," my sister sassed. "Did Dad give you some money to buy your affection, and now you're here to spend it up?"

"At least I'm not selling my body for money," I said to her, truly believing that was not true, but wanting her to understand where I was coming from.

"You want me to give little man here a show?" she teased.

"Ugh, you make me sick," I said, turning Evan around. "Why you gotta take money from those gangbangers? You know they're gonna want you to put out for real, Eva."

"Ella, you moved out. You're breaking Mama's heart, and you gonna tell me what's right about what's wrong? She thinks she not good enough. You gonna try to go and live uptown? You tryna eat off the china? It's already a slap in her face that Dad has a whole other family, and now you are a part of it."

"Please, whatever I do is not as devastating to her as what you're doing. You don't understand. I'm one less mouth for her to feed right now."

Eva said, "Justify it any way you want."

"You know what? I don't even know why I'm here talking to you."

"Exactly, let me shop for you. Here's a perfect little dress that covers up everything."

"You know what? Get out of my face, Eva," I said, pushing her and turning around.

"Evan, come on. Let's go." I looked around the couple of racks, and I did not see my brother there. "Evan? Evan!" I asked the salesperson, "Have you seen a little boy? About three years old with a jeans jumper on and some cute red Converse?"

"Uh-uh," the lazy salesperson replied.

At that point I felt like I was going to pass out. I had no idea where Evan went. I looked all around the store, and he was nowhere.

I turned to my sister and said, "You gotta help me."

I knew she wanted to get smart, but something inside of her would not let her. She said, "All right, come on. We're gonna find him."

When we walked out into the mall, I said, "He wanted the toy store. It's right down there. Maybe he's in there."

"You gotta calm down," Eva said in a reassuring voice.

"How can I calm down? I had the baby and now he's gone. Oh my gosh!"

"Let's just go to the toy store."

I got there before Eva because I ran. I bumped straight into Samantha. "Oh great, I was looking for you guys. I'm starving. Did Evan find something he just couldn't live without ... wait ... where's Evan? Ella, where is Evan?

I stuttered and said, "Um, Evan, uh ..."

"He's in the back of the store," my sister said, trying to have my back.

Samantha asked, "Where's my son, Ella?"

I said, "Well, see what happened was—"

Samantha snapped, "Oh my goodness! You don't know where he is? Evan! I can't believe this. I leave you in charge of him for five seconds, and now he's gone."

"Quit over-exaggerating all of this, lady," Eva said. "He's here. My sister is sick over this. We just started looking for him. He couldn't have gotten that far away."

Samantha gave my sister a mean glare. She rushed to the information booth and got mall security involved. Next thing you know, police officers were there. My sister and I were still desperately trying to find Evan.

"I can't believe you're helping me," I said to her. "Thank you."

A little later, everything inside of me started to fear the worst. When my dad found out I was the reason that his son was missing, I didn't know what I was going to do. We were waiting in the mall's security office when a policeman approached Samantha and said, "We found this shoe. Is it your son's? It was by the exit."

Samantha took one look at it and panicked. When I saw the red Converse, I knew it was Evan's.

She screamed, "Oh no!"

CHAPTER 5

Solidly Intact

I tried to keep it together as the police questioned me about exactly where I was when I first noticed that Evan was gone. Three different officers asked me the same questions. I guess they wanted to see if they could shake me. The thing was, I did not understand why they were being so mean to me. I did not want this to happen. I guess they were trying to find motive because one officer grilled me and asked if I was excited when I found out my dad was having another child with someone else.

Trying to stay calm but being honest, I answered, "No."

"So inwardly you were ecstatic when your stepmother asked you to watch him, because if he got lost it would be one less problem you'd have to deal with," the officer prodded.

"Okay, sir, you're twisting everything around. First of all, she's not my stepmother yet. And second, I've grown to love Evan. Just because I wasn't overjoyed to find out he was on the way doesn't mean I'm not grateful he's here. Why are you sitting here talking to me about nothing, sir? You are wasting time not looking for him."

"Oh, there are people looking for him."

My attention got diverted when I heard Samantha call out, "Calvin."

My dad was here. This was real. I had *lost* my little brother.

Samantha pointed in my direction, "He was with your daughter. I just went to the restroom. I asked her to take him to the toy store. When I got to the toy store, I couldn't find them. I started walking back to the entrance when I saw Ella running toward me. I realized right away that Evan wasn't with her. Then Eva walked in and tried to tell me that Evan was at the back of the store. Calvin, I'm so scared. He's gone, and your fast-tail daughter told me some lie."

I looked over at my sister talking to another officer. I could see in her eyes that she was devastated. Hearing this lady belittle her and not having her father defend her was very hurtful.

I felt the way Eva felt times two. Listening to Samantha bash me cut to the core of my heart, but I couldn't be offended. I had lost her son. If something happened to him, I would never forgive myself.

"You told me to trust her. You told me to give her a chance. I was trying and look where it got me. My baby's gone!" She hit my father in his chest.

"Ma'am, ma'am, we need you to give us a detailed description of what your son looks like," the policeman said to Samantha. "Do you have a photo on your cell phone?"

My dad came over to me. I was ready for him to bite my head off, but I guess he could see I'd already beaten myself up. So he just held me. It was the first time in years I'd ever had my dad comfort me when I was frightened.

"It's going to be okay, Ella. We will find him."

Then I pulled away, realizing I did not deserve his kindness or support. He might not ever see his son again because of me. My irresponsibility was unacceptable.

I said, "Samantha is right. She did trust me. Dad, I was fussing with Eva. I wasn't paying attention to him. I wasn't taking care of Evan the way I should have been. He was pulling on my leg. I knew he wanted to go to the toy store, but I wanted to get an outfit. Oh, Dad, it's all my fault. You should hate me."

"I'm not saying you shouldn't have been more responsible, Ella, but that boy is definitely my son. Every five minutes he is running off somewhere. Last week she lost him in the grocery store. Two weeks before that he ran away from me at the park. As parents, she and I are going to have to tell him he cannot just go where he wants to. She should have told you to watch, watch, watch him."

"Don't blame Samantha, Daddy."

"I'm not blaming her solely. But we all need to share some of the fault. It's not just on you. Right now we need to hope and pray all will be okay. We must stay calm and let the police do their job."

I hugged him so tight. Suddenly, we heard the best sound we could hear.

"Mommy," my little brother screamed, wriggling out of the policeman's grasp and running toward his mother's open arms.

I was so happy everything was going to be all right. Evan was back, and it appeared he didn't have a scratch on him. He was only missing a shoe. What a blessing.

Then I saw two cops bringing a big guy into the mall's security office. My heart sank as I realized it was Leo. What was going on?

One cop said to the sergeant, "We caught this man in the parking lot attempting to leave the mall with the boy."

Leo defended, "I was not leaving. I was going to my friend's car to get my cell phone."

I rushed over to them and said, "Leo, you had Evan?"

"Yeah, I was in the mall. He was crying and looking for you guys. He remembered who I was, and I told him we'd search for you. When I couldn't find you, I knew I needed to call. I left my phone in Amir's car. I couldn't find him either, so I was hoping the car was unlocked. Lil' man and I were headed to the car when these cops just seized me," Leo explained.

"Could you let him go?" I cried.

My dad came over to the sergeant and said, "Sir, I think there must be some mistake. We know this young man."

"No, we have to take him down. You are not able to leave the premises with a child," he stated to Leo. "This boy is not yours. You could have taken the little boy to mall security or used a store phone to call the cops."

I said, "He wasn't going to do anything to hurt Evan."

My dad helped me by saying, "Yes, sir, I can vouch for this young man. He's a football player up at Lockwood High School."

"I don't care if he plays for the Falcons," the stern officer preached to my dad.

"He wasn't gonna hurt Evan. Didn't you just hear him say he was tying to call me? Evan was comfortable with him. He just told you he calmed him down," I said.

A policeman stepped in front of his sergeant and said, "That's how kids get lured to go with an abductor. It's someone they know. It's someone to keep them calm and not make them think anything is wrong. It's someone they like. To take a child off the premises is a crime."

Leo voiced in frustration, "Whatever! Just do what you gotta do."

"No!" I shouted. "I know he wouldn't hurt him."

The sergeant finally started listening. "How do you know that, ma'am?"

Laying it all on the line, I said, "Because this guy you wrongfully have in handcuffs is my boyfriend!"

"Sir, is that true?" the sergeant asked my father. "Were you aware of this? And if so, are you comfortable with your daughter's boyfriend having your son?"

My father paused. He looked at me and could see Leo had my heart. My dad looked at Leo and could tell Leo truly cared about me too. He looked over and smiled when he saw his happy son in one piece. He looked back at the officer and said, "Honestly, I'm completely fine with my daughter's boyfriend being with my son. No problem here, sir."

"Just remember," the cop said, uncuffing Leo, "it is not okay to remove a child from this site when they are not directly in your care."

Leo rubbed his wrists and humbly said, "Thanks. I gotcha."

I hugged him, and we both went over and watched Evan wipe the tears from his mom's eyes. Not having a clue about how worried we all had been, my brother was laughing. My dad told him how scared we were and how important it was for him to never wander away from us again.

"Your boyfriend?" Leo whispered in my ear.

"Yeah, your boyfriend?" my dad asked, coming between the two of us. "Thank you, though, for keeping my boy safe. Take care of my daughter so I won't have to hurt you."

"Yes, sir," Leo replied as they slapped hands.

All was now really right with the world. I'm not saying going through all that was worth it, but in the end Leo became my guy, so it was definitely a nice reward.

Chapter Five

I looked around to thank Eva, but she was gone. I wondered what that was about. However, I was too happy to get upset.

It had only been a couple days since the mall incident. Although in the end things with Evan turned out right, I sensed in Samantha's mind things were still drastically wrong. My dad had already gone to work. She was taking me to school.

On the car ride over when Evan fell asleep, she said, "You know you're not a little girl. As much as your dad would like to try and make up for the time you guys missed, those days are gone. I'm sure you'll agree." I said nothing. "You don't have to respond," Samantha said firmly.

What did she want me to say anyway? I'd apologized to her profusely, I might add. I know this was her son, and I couldn't imagine as a mom how devastated she must have felt going through the whole ordeal. However, it was over. She needed to let bygones be bygones. She would not let up though.

"I'm going to talk to you woman to woman, Ella, because I think you understand more than your dad cares to admit. There's been tension in the house since you have been here. After all you put me through losing my boy, you owe me. I'm pregnant, trying to prepare for this wedding, and I really think it would be best if you moved out."

"What!" I yelled, not realizing that I might wake up Evan.

He immediately started crying. Samantha shot me a look of disgust. I looked away.

"See, this is what I'm talking about. You have no regard for how your actions affect those around you. You think you can do whatever you want. Go on back to sleep, honey," she said to Evan.

When he heard her reassuring voice, he drifted off to sleep. As kind as she was to her son, she was equally hateful to me. Apparently, I was causing her big problems.

"Have you talked this over with my dad?" I asked her, knowing she hadn't. She said I was a lot smarter than she was giving me credit for.

If she ran this by my dad, he would be discussing this with me, not her. She was trying to get me to cut out on my own so she would still be the hero in his eyes. It would be much better for her than my dad thinking she had kicked me out of the house.

"Since you have been here, your father and I have been arguing more. But I can put things back together if you'd just go back over to your mom's. I can make sure we pay you guys a little bit more than we have been. More than what he is supposed to," Samantha stressed.

"You think all I want is money?" I asked, truly upset by her insult.

I didn't know Samantha's story or where she came from. I did not know if her parents were part of her life … If she could even understand how drastically hard it was without both of your parents living under the same roof. I adored having my own room and bath—basically my own space to be left alone—and not worrying about what was in the house to eat or if the lights were going to get turned off. However, I realized I did not want to be someplace where I was so detested.

"I got you," I sighed.

She said some more junk as she took me to school. She said she'd make sure my clothes got home. Also she said I did not have to talk to my dad because she would explain things for me.

She said she knew this was the best thing for everyone involved. Then she stuffed some bills in my hand and turned away from me.

I could not get out of her car fast enough. I put up a wall around myself as I went through the motions at school. I did not speak to my sister or my friends. I was not rude. I just did not hang out where we usually did.

When I got to chemistry class, however, it was hard to shake my partner. We had a lab to do, and Leo could tell I was distant.

"I'm here, just so you know that," he said.

Just as class was ending, it was announced over the intercom that because a severe storm was headed our way, all after school practices were canceled.

"Do you need to go somewhere and talk?" Leo said.

I knew I had the $150 in my pocket that Samantha had given me that morning. There was a hotel down the street, and I impulsively asked Leo to meet me there. I got there first and texted the numbers 2-1-2. I thought maybe I loved him. I did know I cared so much for him and that I wanted him to be my first.

When he came in the door, I immediately jumped on him, put my lips to his, helped him take off his jacket, and lifted up my shirt so I was only in a bra. We made our way over to the bed. He was on top of me, but then he stopped. Leo Steele had a reputation of being a lady's man, so I knew he wasn't scared. Why did he stop?

"Is something wrong with me?" I asked, getting the pillow and covering myself up.

"Ella, you are beautiful. Trust me, the last couple of hours all I been thinking about is getting to this hotel and knocking boots with you. Now that I'm here, I see how vulnerable you are. You are breaking in my arms. That's not what I want from my girl on her first time. What's wrong?"

I just broke down and cried. I told him everything that was going on in my world. Then he held me with such care. He made me feel like he wasn't going to let me break anymore. I actually was not the only one who was dealing with heavy stuff. He opened up to me and told me that the reason why he's been homeless was because his mom just took off and moved to New York to be with some guy. She left him here to fend for himself. Since he was now eighteen, she felt he could do it. Crazy thinking! He had no job.

I said, "We both understand selfish parents. For my mom to let some joker use up money intended for me and my sister was unthinkable."

"I never had a girl that cared for me like you do, Ella. I want to be here for you. You called me your boyfriend and saved me from being arrested. You stuck your neck way out there not knowing how your dad would react."

"I know. That was pretty risky, huh?" I joked. "I didn't even give you a chance to let me know if you really wanted us to be an item."

"I'm not old-fashioned if that's what you are eluding too. I'm not the one who has to ask. If you need to hear me say I want you to be my girl, then there, I said it." He kissed my lips gently. "We'll have our time to take our relationship up another level. Right now it's pretty clear we need to relax and not be stressed. Come here, you!"

Leo brought my body to his. I was so into him. We cuddled under the covers and dozed off.

About an hour later, I woke up and saw him at the desk studying. Bless his heart. He seemed so unsure of what he was doing. I went over and looked at the math and gave him some tips.

"I get what you're talking about," he said after we worked on the problem for a while. "Let me do a couple more problems. Write 'em down; write 'em down."

Leo was so excited that he was getting it. I put my hand over his neck. I was happy. Though my life was not perfect, I had a perfect relationship built on the right thing: truth. I cared about a boy, and I was helping him to be better. Because of my feelings, he could have taken advantage of me, but he was helping me be strong. Maybe I did love Leo Steele. Maybe? Probably. Wow!

I woke up at 10:59 p.m. I was still in the hotel bed. I did not want to move because I was in Leo's strong arms. We both were fully clothed. After we studied, we talked, ordered pizza, and fell asleep. I could not hold back the tears from falling because I thought I had nowhere to go.

I knew my mom practically hated me because I had gone to live with my dad. My dad was probably thrilled that I willingly left his place so I would not continue to cause problems in his life. Where exactly did that leave me?

Well, I now had a boyfriend who I knew would do anything he could to protect me. Problem was, he himself was living with another family. Neither of us had a car. Neither of us had a job. I did not know exactly what I wanted to be. However, I knew I was going to somebody's college, and I had worked hard enough to be able to get a scholarship. Problem was, how I was going to live in the meantime? College was a year and a half away.

I did not want to wake up Leo. I could only imagine that it had to be stressful living with the Strongs. Coach Strong, our head football coach, was known as a tough guy. His son, Blake, used to date my girl Charli. Blake was tired of holding hands and basically found someone else who was willing to give it up. As soon as he broke it off, Charli moved on with his cousin Brenton, who was a super-sweet person. Blake wanted her back. Thankfully, my girl did not choose the smooth operator. Instead, she chose Brenton. She has been happy ever since.

High-maintenance Blake Strong was probably making Leo's life impossible. I had been so busy talking about what was going on in my world that I hadn't asked Leo how he was. As I thought, I moved gently to get out of the bed. He was so in tune with me that he grabbed hold.

Leo said, "You okay? I'm not leaning on you too hard, am I?"

He was six three and a half, two hundred twenty-five pounds. He was heavy, but he wasn't hurting me. It was so sweet that he cared.

"Wait, are you crying?" he asked.

"I'm okay."

"No, you're not, Ella."

"You know it is eleven. Coach Strong is gonna kill you for being out this late," I said. Leo sat up in the bed and crossed his arms. "Leo, why don't you talk to me about what's going on."

"I'm straight. I got it."

"No, you listened to everything I had to say. Now it's your turn. This girlfriend thing is new to me, but I wanna be the best one I can be and not one who you think is so weak that you can't lean on her."

"Blake totaled his car the other night. We don't know if he was drinking or if he fell asleep or what. His car smashed into a tree."

"Omigod! He's okay, right?"

"Yeah, his mom just thinks I'm a bad influence."

"What? What do you have to do with Blake's crazy ways?"

"I know, right? They didn't tell me not to come back, but I gotta figure out something else. I just wish I could take care of you," he sighed.

He wanted to kiss me, but I knew I had been eating pizza from Papa John's with the garlic sauce on it. The last thing I wanted was to steer him away with my ugly breath. I turned my head away and rested it on his chest. Both of us just lay there quiet for a minute.

I knew he was thinking what was next for him. I was doing the same. He was eighteen, and I'd be seventeen in few months. Maybe all we needed to do was quit school and get jobs and try and live.

I blurted out, "We need to get food stamps and subsidized housing. We can make it if we have a baby. We really can."

"Don't play, Ella."

"I'm not playing. We can figure this out. We can't go back to the school and crash. I ruined that by letting Coach know what you were doing," I conceded.

"You saved me by letting Coach know. I'm going to college on a football scholarship, and you're going on an academic one. We can do this. We'll figure out a way to hold on. I'ma go to the front desk and see if they have any toothpaste and toothbrushes 'cause I want a kiss," he said. Then he hopped up, put on his shoes, and headed out the door.

I looked over at my phone. It was on silent. I did not realize I had several messages. Reluctantly, I pushed play.

"Ella, this is your father. I'm on my way to your house. I understand you went back home. I wish we could have talked about this. Just when I'm excited to get close to my little girl before she becomes a grown woman, you're gone. Call your old man back."

I saved that message and went to the next. I heard my mom say, "Ella, where are you? Your dad's here with your clothes. He said you moved back home. It's seven o'clock, but I've not seen you. Where are you, honey? Call us!"

The next was Hallie. "Ella, girl, where are you? Your mom called me. She's even talked to my dad. Do you need to come over here and stay with me? I saw you in school today, and every time I walked your way, you went the other way. Call me, girl! Wherever you are, I'll come get you."

My dad called again and said, "Ella, I'm just leaving your mom's. I waited for an hour. I'm real concerned. Tell us something. Nobody's heard from you."

My mom sounded really upset in the next voice mail, "Ella, baby, it's nine." She called again. "Ella, it's ten. I've been driving around. I'm going crazy. Where are you?"

When Leo came back in the room, I said, "My mom is looking for me. She really sounds panicked." I played her messages for him.

Leo said, "You need to call her right now. And I can get outta here so she won't trip about me being here."

"No, you are going to be safe and stay here tonight. I can have her meet me down the street."

Thirty minutes later, I got in the car with my mom. I was waiting for her to yell and scream and go off. She just held me tight.

"Why didn't you call me?"

"I didn't think you wanted me, Mom!"

"I might get angry with you, girl, but I'll always want you. Now let's go home," she said.

My mom hugged me. I had put up barriers that were not there. Inwardly, I felt joyous. Things with my mom were solidly intact.

CHAPTER 6

Come Correct

Oh, so you guys just wanna quit?" Coach Woods shouted at us at cheerleading practice.

"Might as well because two of our girls aren't eligible," Whitney snarled in Eva and Randal's direction. "And from what I hear about how bad their grades are, even good midterm scores aren't going to help them. So what's the use in us continuing?"

Randal never said a word to anybody, but she stood up and defended, "What are you talking about, Whitney? How are you gonna say what my grades are when you don't even know what I have?"

Whitney got on my nerves. There was nothing wrong with having high expectations, but deliberately picking on people and calling folks out was unnecessary. I looked over at Charli, wanting her to take control. Whitney was not the captain, and a lot of times Charli allowed her to act like she was.

Hallie surprised me when she basically took Whitney's side and said, "I'm just saying if I did all the extra stuff I needed to do to get my tumbling down, then it seems like everyone else needs to take care of their stuff offline too. How can we represent when some members of our team are ineligible?"

"And, Eva, when are you even studying?" Charli asked. "You always want the shortcut. My girl Ella gets in trouble for you, and you don't stand up and take any responsibility."

Eva yelled, "You don't even know what you're talking about."

"Oh, I don't?" Charli stepped toward her face and said. "So you didn't ask her to—"

"Wait, wait, wait, let's not bring any of that up," I intervened.

If Coach Woods found out that Eva was part of the whole cheating scandal, then she would be forced to turn in information that she knew to the administration. While I was not happy about my sister selling me out, I did understand. Also, it was family business.

Trying to be firm, but sweet, I said, "Charli, please just let it go. This has nothing to do with you."

"I don't need you handling anything. I can set Miss High and Mighty straight myself," Eva said to me.

"You can't handle her," Charli said to me. "She hangs you out there to dry. She makes sure she gets away scot-free. And you don't want me to expose her?"

"Since you're so upset with me, then you can have this cheerleading stuff. Bye-bye," Eva said, walking out.

Whitney came over to Charli and said, "Hold on now. Let's be rational about this thing. We can't afford for any of these girls to quit the team. I was just saying what I was saying to motivate them. Charli, you gotta go after Eva."

I was happy to see that a lot of the girls on the cheerleading squad got on Charli. We all were in this together, and while Charli was standing up for me, she did not have the whole story.

Not wanting Charli to get beat up by the squad, I interjected, "Can we take a break, Coach? Everybody's too emotional. Eva's not going nowhere because she does not have a car. We can talk this out."

"I don't understand you," Charli came up to me and said. "Your sister practically spits in your face with her selfish actions and here you are being classic Ella, sweet as pie, forgiving her. For me it is not okay that you were the one in ISS when it should've been her."

"Charli, I love you, girl, and I know you really care about me. However, you think I'm so weak sometimes and that I can't stand up to my own sister. Yeah, we got problems with each other, but we have bigger problems in our household."

"I don't understand. I tell you the deepest things in my life, but yet you're so closed off. I thought we were girls. I thought we were best friends. I didn't even know you had a boyfriend now," Charli huffed.

I looked over at Hallie, who was eavesdropping. I rolled my eyes. She had talked too much.

Trying to soften the blow of me not confiding in her, I whispered, "You and me just haven't talked. And keeping it real, you've been with Brenton twenty-four-seven."

"Whatever! My phone is always on. If you're in any kind of trouble or something, it's not like you called me. Every time I turn around you're always calling Hallie for something. She has to give me the four-one-one."

I looked over at Miss Ray again, and she mouthed "Sorry!" for telling all my business. I motioned for Hallie to come over between the two of us. There was no need to keep all of this a secret. Particularly when Charli knew what was going on in most of my life anyway.

"Look, Charli, I call her all the time," I said, pointing at Hallie, "because it's just her and her dad. I never want to disturb the Blacks. You know how your dad is if you're always on your cell phone. Sometimes the judge can be a little irritable. Bottom line is, my mom has been having a hard time making the rent, and Eva has been doing all kinds of crazy things to help out. She's *trying*, Charli, and you know more than anybody the one thing she loves is cheerleading. Please, let's go find her and talk to her."

Charli nodded. The three of us went out into the hallway. We were all surprised to see Eva on her knees in tears. My sister was always so tough. However, there she sat, destroyed.

She saw us and stood up and yelled, "What are y'all looking at?"

"Just don't quit," Charli yelled. "We need you. Eva, I just wanted to say I'm sorry. I didn't realize y'all had so much going on."

"You never realize it, Charli. You just want what you want and say what you think is right. Like there's only one side to the story." And then Eva stepped to me. "I don't need you trying to make people forgive me. I am who I am, and I'm proud of it. It's none of Charli's business about our family," Eva asserted.

"But I know now and I understand," Charli said. "I know you're having a tough time."

"You shouldn't have to know all of the details to trust me, Charli," Eva said. "Randal, Hallie,

Ella, the three of them might be pushovers, but I'm not, but it seems like when anybody questions your authority, you trip. I knew making you captain was a big mistake. You don't care about the people on the team. You just care about winning. You talk about my bad grades, but when have you offered to study with me?"

Not wanting to be attacked, Charli said, "Yeah, I did. When you were at my house a couple of weeks ago and you were talking about this whole cheating scandal in the first place."

"No, you just said we can all get together and study. You never offered specifically to help me."

Charli said, "Well, why didn't you ask me?"

"What does any of this have to do with anything?!" I screamed at the two of them.

"Eva, if you wanna be mad at me because I told our best friends our business, then that's fine. You haven't been speaking to me, and once I think we're cool, you turn into Dr. Jekyll again."

"I think Mr. Hyde is the bad one," Hallie said.

I screamed back, "Whichever one! The point is, Charli and Eva, that both of you guys are mad, but we all have a mission to win. Let's not quit before we even try. Hallie has been working hard to get her tumbling. Randal's been taking stunting classes to make sure she's able to do her thing at the top of the pyramid. If I'm honest with both of you guys, you always talk about how I'm so sweet, but I never say the truth. Well, Eva, you're a bully. Charli, you're a brat. Both of you guys could use a bite of my sweet apple and mellow out a little bit. Dang."

"I could do that," Charli said surprisingly.

I asked, "Eva, what's it gonna be? You gonna stay with us and not quit? Are you gonna come back into the gym so we can get this team back together and cooperating?"

"Yeah," Eva said.

She did not hug us, but she followed us to the gym. The rest of the afternoon, we practiced harder than we had done in awhile. All twenty of us were about the business of winning, and that is what it was going to have to take. At the end of our excruciating practice, no one said it, but everyone was proud that we did not quit.

I was not panicking, but it had been forty-eight hours since the last time I talked to Leo. I would see him in the hall, but he would walk the other way. I would say his name, but he acted like he could not hear me. I would wait for him after football practice, but he would take forever.

Things at home were a little awkward too. Eva and I shared the same room, the same bathroom, the same refrigerator, the same trash can, but we were not saying anything to each other. I wanted to be able to talk to her and get her advice about how to hold on to my guy. However, I was tired of always being the first one to apologize. I had not done anything. I was the one who had egg on my face for wanting to hang out with my dad and then being pushed aside.

Thankfully, we did not stand near each other in our cheer formation at the football game. We had to get there ninety minutes early to warm up and decorate the gates. I was excited about that because I wanted to go up to Leo and make him talk to me. When I saw him stretching with Brenton, Amir, and two other defensive studs, I went up to my girls, Charli and Hallie, for their assistance.

I said, "Okay, you guys, I need your help."

"What's up?" Charli asked.

"Something's going on with Leo, and I want to talk to him. I know if I go over there alone, it won't work. If Coach looks over and sees the other two guys stretching, it won't be good. If all three of us go over there, then it will seem like Coach Woods told us to go over there and tell the boys something, and Coach Strong would just dismiss it."

"Great! You ain't said nothing but a word. I need to go over to Amir and give him a good luck kiss," Hallie said, shaking her body.

"Settle down," Charli said.

Hallie teased back, "Whatever. You are probably gonna beat me to the punch with Brenton."

"We don't need to make the defensive boys too soft," Charli said. "They need to be strong and get ready to knock some heads, bash somebody, get the ball back, and score."

The two of them went over to their boyfriends. When Leo saw me, he put his hands up in the air. I was not going to let him get away. We had gone through too much for there to be drama.

Finally, looking him eye to eye, I said, "Okay, please talk to me, Mr. Steele. I thought I was being just a little over-the-top thinking you had shut me out, but it's real obvious you don't want to talk to me."

"All right, I was trying not to hurt your feelings, but let me just go out and say it," Leo stated. "I just think it's best if I don't have a girlfriend right now. I thought this could work out between us, but it's just too much."

"What? Am I bothering you too much? I know I left you a gazillion messages, but I was just concerned that everything might not be okay. I didn't mean to push you away," I said, feeling like someone had punched me in the gut.

I stepped up to him, put my hand on his shoulder pad, and stood on my tippytoes because he was a lot taller than me. Leo stepped back. My heart sank.

Not caring I was breaking, he said, "You know what? I gotta go into the locker room. Sorry."

And he was gone. The stands were filling up. Everyone was getting in place. Hallie and Charli had pumped up their guys, so in their world everything was fine. I was the only one shattered. I felt like a tree in the midst of my own winter—leaves and branches bare and shivering with cold. I was nothing but brittle branches, just hanging on. Immediately, I jogged off to the women's restroom. I could sense Hallie behind me.

"Okay, Charli went to go tell Coach Woods where we are, but you gotta talk to me, girl. You wanted to talk to Leo, and now you're upset. What did he say to you?"

"He doesn't want to be my boyfriend, okay? He broke things off."

Hallie embraced me. "Why?" she asked.

I did not want to, but I backed away. I needed her support. I needed her to hold me up before I fell apart. I needed her to tell me that it was all a dream, but I knew there was no need to pinch myself. This was my reality. He did not want me, and I had to accept that.

"Don't worry about it, girl. After the game we are going to talk to him because Amir told me that he really, really likes you. There's gotta be an explanation for all of this."

"I'm not going to beg anybody to be with me," I told Hallie, knowing I had pride and was my mom's daughter and Eva's sister for goodness' sake. "Just when I opened up my heart and thought things were good."

"Well, he ain't the only guy out there. There's more fish in the sea. Plus there's a party tonight, and you can go to it. One thing about being with Leo is you stepped up your game, girl. You don't just wake up and come out the house looking like you used to. You are styling, though I can't figure you and Eva out. You both always complain about not having any money, but every week y'all got on something new."

"Girl, my mom brings us stuff back from Ross, the Body Shop, and TJ Maxx. If you say *sale*, she'll find it."

"I wish I had a mom who cared like that," Hallie lamented.

Oh no. I did not mean to be insensitive to everything Hallie was going through. She just put her mom in rehab, which was a good thing. At least I hoped it was. However, I did not want to open up a can of worms.

Knowing me, Hallie said, "You were wondering about my mom. You didn't put your foot in your mouth. She's doing okay. She's still in there, at least. I remember two years ago my dad put her in rehab, and three days later she was gone. So at least that's not the case. It's been two weeks, and she is still there."

"I'm glad to hear that about your mom," I said to my girlfriend, hugging her tight this time.

Hallie pulled away from the embrace and said, "Listen, I don't know what's going on with Leo, and I know it took a lot for you to trust him. I just really think there's something else going on there that has nothing to do with you. But for now we need to go cheer."

I was a professional cheerleader doing my cheers and my jumps with accuracy. However, my heart was not in it. How could I fully cheer and get behind the Lions when the one who made my heart go pitter-patter had stomped all over it?

After we went on the field at halftime, Hallie came over to me and said, "Come here. Girl, I gotta talk to you."

"What's up?"

"I just talked to Amir before he went into the locker room, and he said Leo feels horrible. It's something to do with the Axes. He just wants you to stay away so you won't get hurt."

"Huh?"

"That's all I know. It's not like he wants to. Give him a couple of days, and when this all blows over, y'all will be fine."

I could not wait for the third and fourth quarter to breeze by. We were playing a horrible team, and we creamed them, 35–7. Leo had three sacks. I saw scouts from Georgia Tech and UGA in the stands.

I dashed over to him and said, "With all your tackles and defensive stand, you're the man."

"Okay, uh, thanks," he said, trying to run around me.

"Leo, I heard about what's going on, something about the Axes. Why does that have anything to do with me? Why does that have anything to do with you? I mean, what's up? Is it Shameek?"

"He's running around telling everybody stuff, and it ain't over between me and him. You and I both know that he doesn't make idle threats. Even if he is bluffing, I can't take that chance." he said. "I'm gonna hang low, and I don't want anybody around me." He lightly cupped my chin in his hand and continued, "Including the girl I really care about.

"I don't want them to think I'm close to you. They're smart enough to know that there's more than one way to hurt me. Ella, if anything happened to you ... You know what? Just stay away."

As I watched him jog to the field house, I did not know whether to be happy or sad. He still really cared about me, and that was great. Unfortunately, the gang we knew to be crazy was not letting go of the drama. So should I do what he said and stay away from him? Following him, I knew there was no way I could.

"Leo, Leo!" I screamed, but he kept going through the field-house door.

Amir and Landon ran up to me. Amir held me back as I tried to go into the locker room. Landon kept pushing his hand downward as if I needed to chill.

Landon said, "People are watching him, Ella. Shameek's got beef with Leo, and all of us are trying to watch his back. We can't watch his and yours too."

"I just don't want him to be scared. I don't want him to be alone. I don't want him to think I don't care. I know the Axes are crazy, but they can't scare us, and I will tell them so."

Landon's eyes widened. "Wait, whoa, hold on, Ella. You need to stay away from those guys. We don't even know if they know that you and Leo … you just need to chill."

"Fine," I wailed, and I rushed over to my girls.

"So where's the party?" Eva said to Hallie.

Hallie shrugged. "I think we better go home. I just talked to some of the guys, and they said things might get crazy with the Axes."

"Shameek and his boys are just talking junk," Eva said dismissively. "Ain't nothing really about to happen. We're on a winning streak, and I'm trying to shake my thang. We don't have to go for a long time, but we need to celebrate. Maybe that's the problem with our team, we don't hang out like we used to."

My sister was slick. She knew the right buttons to push with Charli and Hallie. They wanted us to be a team. If the five of us were going to make that happen, then Charli was all for it.

Our captain said, "All right, maybe just for a little while."

We were always ready for a party. We had on our uniforms, but we had our after-party outfits in the cars. The party was at Wax's house. Like all sets he threw, the place was packed. I stepped into a corner of the living room to get some air. When my phone vibrated, I looked down and was surprised to see a message from Leo.

He texted, "Please tell me that you are not at Wax's."

I wrote back, "Yes, but if you tell me where you are, I can get Hallie to drop me off."

He texted back, "Go home."

I texted back, "Soon."

Just when I was about to go find my girls so we could leave, I was detained. Shameek, the gangbanging idiot, stepped through the door. He licked his lips at me and hissed.

Quickly I said, "Excuse me."

"Oh no, pretty mama, I need to talk to you."

"I'm getting ready to leave," I said, once again trying to get around him.

"Only way you're getting around me, baby, is if you give me some sugar."

"Shameek, please move," I said, trying to push him to the side.

He would not move, so I turned around to find another way out. Two of the Axes were standing behind me. Before I could scream, Shameek had one hand around my waist and the other around my mouth.

He whispered, "I just wanna talk to you, baby. Gotta message I need you to take back to the ole boy."

He held my waist pretty tight, and he was pushing me through the house. The screen door opened, and there were not a lot of people out on the back deck. Shameek took me out that way and down some stairs. It was so dark. My eyes filled up with tears.

"So Steele is your man, huh? I bet you he can't make you feel like this," he hinted. His yucky bad breath made me feel as equally sick as the thought of what he was preparing to do to me.

All I could think of was that Leo told me not to hang out. He told me to stay home. He even texted me and warned me. Why did I have to be such a hard head?

Shameek took his hand off of my mouth. I gasped, "What do you want?"

"I want to hurt your boy. I know if I tap you, it'll be worse than anything I could do to him physically. I know he's such a punk that he probably hasn't even satisfied you yet. You ain't gotta worry, baby. I ain't gonna be gentle, but I ain't gonna take too long. Unbutton her pants, Bruno."

I started screaming. Shameek tried covering my mouth, but I was jerking my head all over the place so that he could not keep me quiet. When he did cover my lips, I bit his hand.

"Can't y'all hold her down? Dang!" Shameek barked.

I just kept screaming, and then I heard Leo call for me. "Ella? Ella?"

"She hasn't left because I'm driving," I heard Hallie say.

"Down—" I screamed before Shameek stuffed something in my mouth.

I heard a bunch of footsteps coming down the stairs. Leo rushed over. Shameek threw me on the ground. I was so scared.

"I wondered where you were, Leo. I was about to have fun and do what you haven't. What? You came to watch?" Shameek teased. "You should have never crossed me when I had business with Blake Strong. You wanna be the hero, but I get the last word."

"You got beef with me, not with my girl."

"Ahh, you told me you didn't have nobody. What? You think I don't have eyes and ears everywhere? That I couldn't find who the trick was who ratted us out when we were bashing your head in? We should've finished what we started back then. Let's finish now."

As Shameek's boy, Bruno, tossed him over a gun, Amir yelled, "Leo, watch out!"

"No!" I screamed. I darted toward Leo to get him out of the way, but the shot rang out and the bullet hit me.

"No!" I heard Leo howl. I felt him catch me as I fell.

People were running. People were screaming, and I was losing it. My body felt cold. I was in pain. I saw his concerned face looking down at me. He was crying as he held me close. My limp body did not feel so bad.

"Stay with me," Leo begged. "Come on, Ella, stay with me. I love you, girl. Please don't leave me. Call the ambulance!"

I tried, replying, "I … I …"

I wanted to tell him that I loved him too. However, I could barely breathe. I wanted to tell him not to cry, but I wanted to cry. I wanted to let out tears of joy that he was okay. I wanted to tell him not to ever break up with me again. Whatever was going on in our lives, we could get through it together. As I became woozier, I thought that maybe this was my end.

Once again I tried to speak. "Love … love …"

Leo said, "Don't talk. Don't talk now, Ella."

"Love you," I forced out. "Where … Eva?"

Leo said, "Shhh, we'll find her."

I knew I loved Leo, and I knew I had to show him he was not alone. As my eyes closed, I knew that he knew I loved him. I did not intentionally take the bullet, but when you love somebody, you try to protect them. Instinct takes over. Though it might have cost me my life, I had come correct.

CHAPTER 7

Joyous Screams

When I opened my eyes, the ceiling was the first thing I saw. I realized I was on my back. Turning my head to the left and right, I noticed how everything looked so sterile. I tried hard to figure out what was going on. Then I remembered I had been shot.

Seeing all white, I wondered if I was in heaven, but as I heard my mother scream, I knew differently. "*You* did this to her. What have you done to my baby?"

I heard Leo's voice reply. "I'm so sorry, ma'am. I'm so sorry."

I realized maybe I was in hell because my mom was hitting my boyfriend repeatedly like he had pulled out the gun and shot me himself. I had to get up, but the pain in my arm and the wooziness in my body would not let me move.

"Just get out. I don't want her around you *ever*. You put my baby in harm's way. She could die."

Witnessing my mother being too harsh, a nurse walked in and said, "Ma'am, I don't think your daughter's going to die from getting grazed by a bullet. Let's not exaggerate."

"Is she gonna be okay?" Leo asked the nurse in a very caring tone.

The lady replied, "Yes, she is a lucky girl."

I was unable to sit up because my shoulder was hurting profusely. "Ow!" I moaned.

"My baby, Ella, oh, sweetheart," my mom cried, rushing to my side when she saw I was conscious.

Having her close, I got on her. "What are you saying to him, Mom?"

"I'll let you guys talk," Leo said. He was backing away and going toward the door.

"No! Please, Mom, don't let him go. I love him," I admitted.

"What?" she marveled.

Leo said, "It's okay, Ella. Your mom has a point. You should not have been there."

"No, Leo. My mom needs to know the whole truth," I said, struggling to talk. "This is the guy you cooked the food for, Mom. This is Leo. I've cared about him for a while. He told me not to come around. It's those stupid gang members who did this, not him."

My mom questioned, "Well, how and why did you get shot, girl?"

"They were after me, ma'am," Leo stepped up and admitted.

"Exactly. Stay away from her," my mom said bluntly to Leo.

"No, no, Mom. I ran in front of him so they wouldn't shoot him. He pushed me away so the bullet wouldn't actually hit me. We were trying to protect each other."

"You gotta believe me, Ms. Blount. I didn't want any of this to happen. You best believe I'ma take care this though," Leo growled.

"Oh no you're not, son. The police is gonna have to get involved," my mom declared.

"No, Mom, 'cause then the gang is gonna come after us."

"They have already come after you. We are gonna get the whole community involved in this thing: your principal, Pastor King, other leaders, everyone. You guys are too young to ruin your future or to have your future stripped away by senseless violence," she affirmed.

"Leo, that's your name, right?" my mom said to the guy I cared for so deeply. "I'm sorry. I'm just a protective mama who wants the best for her baby. Thank you for caring."

"I do care, Ms. Blount. I care a lot."

"I believe that, baby. Eyes don't lie. Ella ain't never liked nobody. She said she loves you, and I respect that. Now it makes sense. You're the boy she had me cook the extra food for. I knew she liked that guy—well, *you*—because she was trying to tell me how to cook. She wanted everything to be just right," my mom joked. Then she looked at Leo square in the eyes. "Promise me you not gonna retaliate. If you do, you are no better than the one who shot my baby."

Leo looked away. My mom's gentle hands turned his face back toward her. She was very serious.

"Promise me," she said.

"I promise," he finally agreed.

"Great! I'll be right back. We can't stay in here too long. Ella needs to get some rest."

When my mom left, Leo rushed over to me. "I want to hug you, but I don't want to hurt your arm."

"Hold me, please," I said, shaking a little.

I wanted to yell out, "Yeah, I'm okay. Yeah, my mom has given me and Leo a chance. Yeah, I love him, and yeah, he loves me back," but I just let him hold me.

"You know my mom is right. You can't be taking matters into your own hands, Leo. You can't think you're a bulletproof vest."

"Ella, what would I have done if he would have killed you? You should have hit the deck."

"I didn't want you to get shot."

"Better me than you," Leo responded.

"No, I could not stand it when I saw you in this hospital a couple weeks back."

He touched my face and said, "And you think this is a picnic for me, coming to visit you here?"

I teased, "At least we know we are a match for each other. We can't stay out of the emergency room, huh?"

"Yeah, well, we don't need to be back here again. I'm not gonna live my life afraid. I promised your mom I wouldn't go after those guys, but ..." Leo shook his head. "What am I gonna do with you, girl?"

"Love me," I said, remembering he said that before I got shot.

He kissed my forehead. "How could I not love you? You turn in work for me. You make sure I eat. You make sure I don't get my head bashed in. You make sure I don't get shot."

"Yeah, but you pushed me out of the way, and you're here to make sure I'm okay."

"I guess you're stuck with me," Leo said.

When the door opened, Leo stood up. My mom came in with two policemen behind her. They questioned us, and we did not hold back. The Axes were nobody to mess with. Things had already escalated out of control. Somebody had to stop the bleeding. Everyone was so horrified about what had happened that my mom said our friends at the party had already given their account to the police. If we all stood together, maybe the Axes would be dissolved for good.

"I have all I need for now," the officer said to me. "You're a very lucky lady. It's nice to see teens sticking together. Truly, the only way were are going to get crime off the streets is if you all do what's right and face these monsters who think they can control us. Then we can all be free."

"Just make this a priority," my mom said.

"We are going to do our part to take care of this," the officer assured her.

"You better," she said.

While my mom talked to them at the door, Leo came over and said, "Get some rest."

"My mom's feisty, huh?"

"She cares about you."

"I'm glad she knows I care about you," I said to him.

"I love you, Ella Blount," he whispered. I repeated his words in my head over and over and over before I fell asleep.

The next day I was released from the hospital and back at home. "You're okay?" my sister asked. "I know you hate me. I've been such a jerk to you. I don't know what I would've done if you died. It's like the better half of me would have been gone. Why did you step in front of that bullet?"

"It was an accident, but it's not like I had a lot to live for," I blurted out.

Both my mom and my sister looked stunned. I was serious. My life had been super hard the last couple of weeks.

I explained, "Things have been messed up around here. Eva, you and I have been walking around in the same space not even speaking to each other. Mom, you work so hard you didn't know how depressed I had been."

"Here, come to this couch and sit down," my mom said. "I need to talk to both of you girls. Eva is right, Ella. There is no way I'd be okay if you weren't here. You know I watch the news daily, and there's always somebody losing their child. I grip my heart every time, feeling for what they are going through. Well, I made some bad choices. I don't want to lose you." Eva looked away. "And, sweetheart, I don't want to lose you either."

Eva smiled. I knew that my tough and sassy twin felt things deep down. I was happy to see her feel love.

"You guys both know Trevon took me through a lot of turmoil. I was searching for love and wanted it so badly that I accepted anything. It was like I was in a daze. When I finally woke up, I got rid of his tail. But a lot of damage had been done. I knew it wasn't a burden you girls should have to shoulder, so I didn't tell you about it. I thought if I worked double shifts and picked up extra jobs, I could put back some of the money I let him waste away."

"Mom, why didn't you just tell us?" I asked.

"Yeah," Eva responded. "We knew Trevon was no good."

"It wasn't right for me to let you guys think your dad wasn't holding up his end of the deal. I was bitter and mad at him for leaving. However, I tricked him back in the day. I don't like saying I got what I deserved, but he wasn't in love with me. The kind of woman he wanted is the kind of women he's with now, someone educated, petite, a more polished lady. I could have been that girl, but I got lazy and didn't wanna work hard. Eva, you remind me a lot of myself, girl, so full of potential, but you think the world is against you. Ella, you care so much about other people, but you have to know when you're being too kind. You can't put yourself in front of a bullet."

"I know, Mom," I said, replaying the event in my mind and not believing what I had done.

"I guess I just want both of you girls to know I love you so much, and I want you to be better than me. Make better choices. I been going to work and trying to further my education. I enrolled in technical school. I want to become a nurse. I can't push you and tell you to be all you can be when you have a mama who hasn't reached her own dreams and goals. Your education is important, too important for anyone to come and copy your knowledge," my mom said, glaring at me.

I responded, "I understand."

"I hope you do," she replied. Then she looked at my sister and said, "You are too important not to get an education. People don't pay people in this world who know nothing. They pay for education. So go and get yours, or you gonna wake up one day and regret that you didn't try harder, be better, and excel."

This was the first heart-to-heart my mom had had with us in years. Eva appeared to be taking it in. I did the same.

"I'm going to go cook. Your boyfriend wants to come by and check on you. I figured I better make a nice meal. I know he can eat," my mom joked.

She went to the kitchen. Eva sat down beside me. I hoped we could work out our differences.

"I'm sorry," she said. "I put you in ISS."

"You had good reason."

"Yeah, but I could have let you in on it. I could have made sure your paper was not left to be caught, and honestly, I should have come up with another plan. Mom is right. I gotta apply myself more."

"I can help you," I said, knowing my sister's grades were in trouble.

"You're really not mad at me? 'Cause Charli and Hallie are."

"Yeah, but they don't live in this house, and they don't know how you have been trying to hold things up around here."

"Leo Steele, huh?" my sister teased. "You didn't get my permission to talk to him."

"I'm growing up, huh? For real, though, can I push you with school, and you not take it personally?" I was real happy when Eva nodded.

"Good, 'cause you know I love you. If I can get As, you can get As too."

"I love you too," she affirmed.

When someone knocked on the door, Eva looked at me and said, "Ahh, Leo is crazy about you. I thought he told mom he'd be here later on."

I started fixing my hair. Eva gave me a thumbs-up. She opened the door. Both of us were stunned to see our father.

"Eva, can I please come in?"

Eva turned back and looked at me. We had not talked about why I left my dad's place. Thankfully, my mom did not push me for details. She knew it wasn't good though.

"It's fine," I said.

I had just gone through a completely tough ordeal. A bullet had hit a part of my body. It was a blessing that I was still here. If my dad came all the way over to make sure I was okay, the least I could do was speak to him.

"Who is that?" my mom said. She walked into the family room, drying her hands. "Oh, hey, Calvin."

"Erika," my dad replied, handing my mom an envelope. "I just wanted to give you something."

My mom asked, "What's this?"

"Just help for the rent. Our girls need to be stable. You don't need to be this stressed."

"Why you doing this?" she asked. "We were actually just talking about you. I told the girls I ruined things, not you."

He said, "Sometimes we have people in our life who do stupid things. They need grace and so do we."

My dad wasn't making sense. It seemed like he was holding back. However, I was so happy he was blessing us.

"I know you are resting, pumpkin," my dad came and said to me. "And I'm just so happy you are okay. Your mom called and told me there was a shooting. I can't explain how awful I felt to get that news. Samantha felt pretty bad too." I looked at him in a strange way. "I know, right? 'Cause when she came clean and told me the real story of why you left so abruptly, she and I decided that maybe the lavish wedding we were planning could be scaled back so I could really help my family."

"Why did you leave?" Eva asked.

"She didn't tell you?" my dad asked.

"She's a sweet girl who doesn't cause rifts," my mom said to my dad before looking at me. "She didn't say anything. Do you want to now?"

"Samantha just told me it would be better if I was gone. Me being there was causing tension. So instead of being a problem for Dad, I left," I uttered.

My dad said, "For the longest time Samantha kept telling me she didn't know why you were gone. But that wasn't the case, and she finally confessed. I realized we can all be with people who sometimes influence us the wrong way. I thought about Trevon, and I'm sorry for being so judgmental. You did a great job with our girls, Erika. And Miss Eva is a spitfire just like you. I love you both, and you're welcome to my home anytime."

I tried to get up to hug my dad, but my wound needed time to heal. He bent down and kissed my cheek. Eva was reserved with him, but she wasn't mean. That was a blessing. My immediate family was still very dysfunctional, but we were coming together.

I just shouted out. "I love y'all."

"All of you guys did not have to come over here!" I bawled. My sister had planned an impromptu get-well party.

I would have been fine just chilling with Leo, but Eva had Charli, Randal, Hallie, and some of the football players over as well. The boys went all out. Blake Strong gave me flowers. Brenton brought me candy. Landon gave me one of his dad's new books. Amir gave me a card.

"Dang, y'all making me look bad. I should have gotten her something," Leo joked.

"You've given me yourself. Just you being here means more than you know," I noted.

We got to talking about grades. I told Eva, Randal, and Leo to come closer when I noticed the three of them were not as confident as the rest of us were. Clearly, they needed help with their academic performance.

"We've got two big tests coming up in math as well as in US History. I will rest now. Tomorrow after church, I'm gonna help the three of you guys for a couple of hours. Next week after cheerleading and football practice, we're going to study, study, study. If you guys give me a chance to help you, I promise you're gonna do well."

The three of them gave me unhappy looks and grumbled. I knew if people weren't used to studying, it was not going to be something they saw as exciting. For me, studying was my friend. When my teachers taught something I didn't know, I would take the book and read the chapter. If I still did not get it, I reread the chapter. I also made notes on what I read. If it was my workbook, I highlighted the important parts. Another one of my tricks was asking the teacher to go over what I missed on tests when I did not score one hundred percent. I'd keep old tests to use as study guides. Therefore, when the exam came, I would not have forgotten all I had learned. These small things added together made all of the difference.

I actually had three good students who came in Sunday, ready to get to work. We spent one hour working on math. The second hour we worked on American history. Since we were all in after-school activities and had forty minutes between the end of school and practices, we could work on the books then as well.

Everyone was surprised to see me at school Monday morning. My arm was in a sling, but I was feeling better. Since I didn't need to, I did not want to miss school.

"This week flew by. You're an amazing teacher," Leo said to me Thursday evening. "I'm actually ready to take the tests tomorrow. I feel like I will do a great job."

"Well, I think the difference is you want to learn."

"I've always wanted to learn, but some teachers just don't try to make sure I get it."

"Yeah, but I have been in class with you, and you get frustrated. You had no problem making sure I explained it in a way that you understood."

"Yeah, but none of my teammates were around to rag me for not getting it the first time, or second time, or third time," he tried rationalizing.

That was not working with me, and I held my ground and said, "You're a big, strong football player. Since when did you care what your teammates think?"

"You got a point. How's that arm?"

"I go to the doctor tomorrow, but I feel good."

"You heard, right?"

"What? About Shameek?" I asked.

"Yeah, and about six other Axes."

"Yup. They were arrested. Two are in jail and four are in juvenile detention."

Leo said, "It isn't cool brothers got their life messed up like that, but I'm pretty happy about the arrests. Time to put all this gang stuff behind us."

Telling him all I'd heard, I said, "Word's out, they will be recruiting sometime soon. Just don't let it be you."

"Me joining the Axes? *Please*. I am worried about my boy, Landon, though. He's talking some crazy junk."

"Well, help him stay clear of those fools going nowhere fast," I said.

At the cheer competition, things were different. Ella and Randal were able to compete because they had done well on their testing and gotten their GPAs up. Unfortunately, I wasn't able to perform because of my arm. However, I was sitting in the stands wearing the cutest Lockwood Lions' competition cheer squad shirt. And I was not sitting alone. Several members of the football team were around me. A lot of our parents had decided to come to this competition, and they were sitting with me too.

When our squad went out onto the floor, we had so much spirit. The gym was shaking. Because we had already switched up the routine, it was easy for the girls to show out without me participating. Nothing bobbled, moves were crisp, and the tumbling was on point. The difficulty we added to the routine stood out. There were eight squads in our division. We had a chance to place. The same squads who had dominated us and looked down on us were smiling in my direction.

The announcer, who I did not know, called me on the loudspeaker to come to the center of the floor. Leo helped me up. I stood there with my team behind me.

The announcer said, "Miss Ella Blount, on behalf of all the cheerleaders in this competition today, we present you with a bouquet of roses. We heard about the awful shooting, and we are truly thankful you are okay. While this is a competition, there is still camaraderie and a bond among those competing."

I looked over at my parents who were supporting us as a unit for the first time ever. I smiled. I looked over at my sister and girlfriends who were holding hands and happy for the first time in a long time. I smiled. I looked at my boyfriend in the stands with the other football players. They were excited we did well, and it made me smile.

I thought about the fact that I had helped Leo, Randal, and Eva understand that hard work pays off. I was a sweetheart and sometimes a knucklehead. I had learned so much in a few weeks. If you really truly care about people, you needed to stand up and help them do the right thing. You have to be willing to let them fall on their own if they don't want to do right.

It was hard being a teen, but I could make it easier by doing my part. I was still here for a reason, and I wasn't going to waste a day. My team wanted me to sit with them as we waited on the floor for the results. When it was announced that we won second place, we were as excited as if we'd taken first. Everyone who came to cheer on the Lockwood Lions let out joyous screams.

STEPHANIE PERRY MOORE is the author of many YA inspirational fiction titles, including the *Payton Skky* series, the *Laurel Shadrach* series, the *Perry Skky Jr.* series, the *Yasmin Peace* series, the *Faith Thomas Novelzine* series, the *Carmen Browne* series, the *Morgan Love* series, and the *Beta Gamma Pi* series. Mrs. Moore speaks with young people across the country, encouraging them to achieve every attainable dream. She currently lives in the greater Atlanta area with her husband, Derrick, and their three children. Visit her website at www.stephanieperrymoore.com.

WANT A DIFFERENT
point of view?

JUST *flip* THE BOOK!

LOCKWOOD LIONS

The Lockwood High cheer squad has it *all*—sass, looks, and all the right moves. But everything isn't always as perfect as it seems. Because where there's cheer, there's drama. And then there are the ballers—hot, tough, and on point. But what's going to win out—life's pressures or their NFL dreams?

BALLER
Swag

Leo Steele is the toughest
thug in school—and football is his life.
But when life gets tough, will football win?

DO YOU

Stephanie Perry Moore
& Derrick Moore

SADDLEBACK
EDUCATIONAL PUBLISHING

BALLER SWAG

All That

No Hating

Do You

Be Real

Got Pride

SADDLEBACK
EDUCATIONAL PUBLISHING
www.sdlback.com

ISBN-13: 978-1-61651-886-8
ISBN-10: 1-61651-886-3
eBook: 978-1-61247-620-9

Printed in Guangzhou, China
0612/CA21200872

16 15 14 13 12   1 2 3 4 5

To both Mr. and Mrs. Steve Shadrach &
Mr. and Mrs. Jim Sanders (Derrick's Mentors)

We have continuously been able to soar because of your help. Thanks to you opening your homes and hearts, we have been able to make a difference in this world. You have been a role model for us on how to do life big. What a blessing to have you care so much.

You are magnificent people ... we love you!

ACKNOWLEDGEMENTS

When you have big dreams, you have to be committed to making them come true. You have to aggressively equip yourself with the skills needed for your journey. You cannot be lazy. You cannot rest. You cannot underestimate those who are working hard as well because they also want your dream. If you find yourself going backwards, don't blame your circumstances, blame yourself.

So what you might not have the best home life, be the smartest, or have finances to make your way easier. You have a mind and you have drive. Use what you have to gain everything you want. Make wise choices. Message we want you to grasp: a genuine baller is "the man" because he works at it, takes nothing for granted, and seizes all opportunities. Set out to accomplish greatness. You are capable of that and much more. Do you.

Here is an enormous thank you for all who help us "do" well.

Acknowledgements

To our parents: Dr. Franklin and Shirley Perry Sr., and Ann Redding, because you stood steadfast and did your jobs as great parents, we had a chance to do remarkable things.

For my publisher, especially my editor, Carol Pizer, because you embraced the writing, we have a chance to help young people reach their dreams.

To our extended family: brothers, Dennis Perry and Victor Moore, sister, Sherry Moore, godparents, Walter and Marjorie Kimbrough, young nephews, Franklin Perry III, Kadarius Moore, and godsons, Danton Lynn, Dakari Jones, and Dorian Lee, because of your love, we are able to write stories that hopefully will help others love themselves.

To our assistants: Joy Spencer and Keisha King, because you all did your jobs, we were able to do ours.

To our friends who mean so much: Paul and Susan Johnson, Chan and Laurie Gailey, Antonio and Gloria London, Chett and Lakeba Williams, Jay and Deborah Spencer, Bobby and Sarah Lundy, Harry and Torian Colon, Byron and Kim Forest, Donald and Deborah Bradley, because you are there for us, we are able to be there for others.

To our teens: Dustyn, Sydni, and Sheldyn, because you are our growing babies, we love so much, and we work hard daily to show you the way.

To the media specialists, school administrators, teachers, and educational companies across the country who support us, especially the great folks in Atlanta Public Schools, because you allowed us to work with your great students, we were able to pen this cool series that we hope will bless many.

To our new readers who we believe will reach their goals. Because you have passion, you can do anything but fail.

And to our Lord, who has blessed us with this opportunity to create and help. Because You have given us a desire to help struggling readers, we hope we are making you proud.

CHAPTER 1

Move On

Lions we're 3–0," Coach Strong said to us in the locker room after the football game. "And I'm so proud of each and every one of you. You've been digging deep. You've been stepping up. Individually, you've been covering your assignments. And collectively, we've been stellar. I'm proud of your effort."

"So, Coach, do we get tomorrow off? No film, right?" Waxton, our star running back yelled out.

"We wanna make it 4–0, don't we?" Coach yelled back. "I'll see you all tomorrow at eleven. Head on out to the buses so we can get back to the school. Steele, I need to see you real quick."

"Yes, sir, Coach," I said immediately, going to see the man I admired.

I had no clue what Coach wanted from me. I had a pretty good game. Two sacks, a forced fumble, six tackles, two for a loss, and seven assists. Heck, he should have been giving me the defensive player of the game award. I would have thought there was something positive he wanted to talk to me about, except the way he called my name with irritation let me know he was not pleased with Leo Steele.

"You wanted to see me, Coach?" I asked.

"You played a tremendous game tonight, son."

"Thanks, Coach."

"But I got a problem."

"Yeah, Coach?"

"I've been checking in with all the teachers, asking them to let me know if any of my players are failing. Right now you are failing math and history. Boy, what are you doing? Sleeping in class?" he lectured. "Midterms are coming up. Unless you want to be sitting on the sidelines and cheering like the girls with pom-poms, you'd better get it together. Am I making myself clear? If you need a tutor, open your mouth. No, no, I take that back. There's gonna be mandatory

tutoring for the next couple of Saturdays in the school library. You be there."

Not wanting to go, I asked, "Tomorrow? We got practice, Coach."

"We're watching film at eleven. Tutoring is at ten. Go there for an hour and then come on to practice. I just don't get it with you, Steele. You're one of my most aggressive players. You go get it on the field. You know what you want to do, and you handle your business. Aren't you trying to play D1 ball?"

"Yes, sir, Coach."

"Well, they don't take idiots. So if that's your goal, if that's what you're trying to do, then I suggest you get on your work. It's like when you double team. You get down low, and you put more into it and make sure you quickly get off your blocks. If the subject is hard, then you got to put more into it as well. No excuses. If the grades don't come up, you're off the team."

On the bus ride back to Lockwood High School, my teammates were fired up. Inwardly, I, too, was excited we were 3–0. We knew we had a great team. We were good on offense and

defense. However, since I got lectured, I was not as excited as they were. How was I going to get *me* together? Being taken out of the starting line—that was not an option.

"So you gonna hang out with us or what, man?" Landon asked when we got back to his car in the school parking lot.

"Nah, dude, just take me home."

"Why? There are a couple of sets we need to fly by."

"Man, I need to go study."

"On a Friday night, Leo, really? You're talking to me."

"Coach just told me if I don't handle my business, I am going to be watching y'all play. So, uh, take me home."

"Dang, I didn't know it was like that. Let me get you there quick. We need you on defense."

On the ride to my place, it was a little quiet in Landon's car. For a preacher's kid, he tried hard to be a bad boy. He'd have his music blaring, and it was not gospel. It was hardcore nasty rap, but now the music was off.

"What's up with you, man? I haven't seen Pastor King at any of the games."

"I know, right? He says he's my number-one fan, and he wants me to get out there and do my thing. Yet every Friday night, he's out of town speaking somewhere trying to save some soul but forgetting about his own son. You know what I'm saying?" Landon disdained.

Finally, we reached my apartment and I got out. "Man, just talk to him. Go home tonight."

Landon's dad was not the only parent who had not come to our games this year. My mom was absent as well. Ever since she found the wrong dude to whisper the right things in her ear over the summer, she had been wanting to be with him more than me. When I opened the front door and walked inside, I did not know how interested in him she was until I saw both of them there packing everything.

"Mom, what's going on?" I hollered.

"Calm down, Leo, let me explain," she said, rising from wrapping glass in newspaper.

I asked, "What are you guys doing? Tell me we're not moving in with him."

"Leo, this is my boyfriend, Frankie. Well, he's wanted to meet you lots of times, but with your football schedule it's just been impossible."

Frankie stuck out his hand trying to impress my mom, but I would not shake it. I looked at it as if it had cyanide on it. I felt if I touched it, my hand would dissolve away or something. I mean, here was this man helping my mom pack up our place, and I didn't know anything about it.

"Mom, what's going on?"

She said, "The little job I have here is not going to advance me forward. Frankie feels—"

Cutting her off, I huffed, "Frankie feels? Who cares what *he* feels?"

Frankie stepped to me and said, "Hey, watch your mouth with your mom, son."

"I'm not your son," I scoffed.

My dad died when I was in elementary school. I was actually with him. We were in a bad car accident, and he did not make it. At the time, I did not know much about adult things. I kept hearing my mom cry at night, saying she did not know how we were going to make it. I always respected the fact that she did not get with any old joker to help her pay bills. So now I was surprised this Frankie guy had influence over her.

"Leo, calm down and step back."

The little shrimp my mom was with might have thought he was tough, but I could take him. I was six three and a half, two hundred twenty-five pounds. He looked to be about five eight, one sixty-five tops. I could snap him.

"Mom, I'm not moving in with this guy. Where does he live anyway? I gotta stay in this school zone so that I can play for the Lions. We're going to win state."

"Y'all have only won three games. I think it's pretty premature of you to talk about how y'all gonna win state," Frankie offered.

"Come on, this is insulting," I said to my mom. I'll bet that jerk probably wished he played back in the day. I completely ignored him.

Frankie got in my mom's face. "He is not coming with me. No way. I'm not taking care of any grown man. No way."

"Frankie, let me talk to him," my mom said, trying to calm the guy down.

"Mom, what is he talking about? You can't go somewhere without me."

The look on Frankie's face spoke volumes. The sly way he held his lips and the chuckle he had in his voice told me I was wrong. My mom

was planning to move in with some man she had not even known for six months and leave her son. I looked at her like, *You gotta explain this*.

Her eyes were watering as she said, "Okay, I know you probably think this doesn't make a lot of sense, but I just need a fresh start. I need to get away, and you're eighteen. You have so much invested here. I'm going to move to New York with Frankie. I'm going to be able to send some money back to you. I just got to get away, Leo. You'll be okay."

I shook my head and walked down the hall to my room and slammed the door. My bed was gone. I did not understand this, but with the long away game, an equally long ride home, tough talk with the coach, and now finding out that my world was turning upside down, I didn't care. I was exhausted. I curled up on the floor. My plan was to deal with all of this the next day.

Coach was going over film in the team meeting. I was so glad that I had a good game the night before because whatever he was saying was going in one ear and coming out the other. It was not that I was not trying to figure out how

I could be better because I did miss a couple of assignments. However, I took his criticism like a man; but honestly, I had bigger fish to contend with. At the moment I was drowning in uncertainty and letting the worry get the best of me. How was I going to take care of myself? Yeah, I heard my mom talk a good game about sending some money back to me. However, our apartment was $650 a month. While the government paid for half of that, I could not even afford $325.

"Steele, are you listening?" Coach Strong called me out.

"Yes, sir."

He asked, "What'd I just say, man?"

And the whole team laughed at me because I could not repeat his critique. Coach Grey was a sweet older gentleman and our defensive coordinator. Though he was a white dude, he could keep the brothers in line. When Coach Grey called me out of the team meeting, I immediately went into defense mode.

"I'm sorry, Coach, I just got a lot on my mind. I know it seemed like I was asleep, like I wasn't paying attention. I was in it. You know I wanna get better."

"No, no, Steele. I just wanted to let you know your mom wants to see you. She's in the parking lot."

"Oh, okay. Thanks, Coach. I'll be right back."

Immediately I thought I'd been stressing for nothing. Finally, my mom came to her senses and did not want to wait until I got home to reverse the idiotic junk she told me the night before. However, when I got outside and saw a U-Haul hitched to the back of her car and the jerk, Frankie, driving it, my stomach got queasy.

My mom stood out with her arms open wide. The sick feeling in my gut intensified. She was about to be out.

"Dang, Ma, I thought we had some time."

"Well, you saw me packing up last night, Leo. There's no need to prolong this. I really need to try to start over. Frankie has a job waiting for me up North."

"What kind of job, Mom? What does he have that you can't do down here?"

"Management at a hotel. I've been cleaning houses all my life, and now I can be over ladies doing it in one of those big, fancy-schmancy, high-dollar hotels. I got to try it, sweetie, and if I

could take you with me, I would. I wanted to give you this money." She opened my hand and said, "It's not a lot."

I looked down at about seventy dollars. That was definitely not a lot.

"Also, here's the thing ... here are all of your clothes, baby," she hesitated, pointing to the back of the car. "Frankie's getting them now."

"You could've just left them. I know I gotta get my own furniture and stuff because you leased all my furniture."

"Well, I couldn't tell you last night, baby, because you were so upset, and you left out and—"

"What else, Mom? What else is there to let me know?"

"I don't have the apartment anymore. You can't stay there, sweetie."

"So where am I suppose to live?"

Frankie handed me my clothes in an old army bag. "That's your problem to figure out, big man."

"Mom, are you serious?" I said, wondering what was wrong with her.

I always came first in her life, but she was acting as if the digits one and eight put together

meant that she did not have to take care of her son any longer. While I was growing up, my life had lots of desires and needs. I felt her decision was a horrible one. Yet I knew my place. I was still a kid. I was her kid. She did not raise me to talk back. My smart mouth was for the streets. Why didn't she care? I wanted to shake her and punch him.

"Look, I'm still going to be paying for your cell phone. I'm going to be calling and checking up on you. I know you'll figure it out," she sobbed.

"We need to get on the road," Frankie said, pulling my mom back to the U-Haul.

But her feet were firmly planted, like she did not want to leave. I put my arms around her tight. I hoped she would feel my heartbeat against her, and we would have a connection again and that our bond would cause her to stay.

"Oh, this is going to be so hard. I love you, Leo. All that I taught you, remember it. You're a good boy. Be better than me," she said. She quickly got into the car and shut the door.

It was just me and Frankie standing there. Man to man our body language spoke volumes. We did not like each other. He had my mom though.

"Don't look so sad," he joked.

"You had better take care of my mama," I threatened.

He walked back to the driver's side, looked back at me, and grinned, "Oh, I'ma take real good care of her."

He laughed. I was in a pickle. At least I did not have to worry about how I was going to pay the rent; I had no place to live. Of course this posed another problem. Where was I gonna stay?

When practice was over, Coach Strong asked to see me in his office. I hid my army bag. I did not want anyone asking me any questions.

"What's wrong, Steele? Is everything all right with you and your mom? She's never come up here and interrupted practice before. Talk to me."

I was looking all around his office, too prideful to look him in the eye because I did not want him to see what I was going through. What I was about to say was an absolute lie.

"Everything's fine," I whispered.

"Good, good. Sit on down and let me talk to you. I love my couch," Coach said out of the blue. Then he got real comfortable.

When I sat down on it, I agreed. It was plush. He had a blanket on the other end. His office had a refrigerator with some snacks. There was a shower here. He had a TV in his office. Luckily, Coach didn't know why it mattered that I thought it was so comfortable, but I realized at least until I figured out my situation, I was going to have to squat at the school.

"All right, well, if you are all right, get on out so I can lock up."

"Uh, Coach, do you mind if I watch a little bit more film? My mom will be back to get me. I know how to lock up."

Coach looked at me like he was trying to size up my character and nodded. "Yeah. That's cool."

I knew he was not supposed to leave me there. While I hated lying, I had to do what I had to do. Fall was in full throttle in the ATL. Though it was warm in the day, it would dip to the forties and fifties at night. A brother could not just be on the streets.

An hour later, I settled really good into my new temporary home. I found a place for my clothes in a locker no one used. I just needed to get into the shower and unwind.

While under the hot water, the reality that I was now homeless and practically an orphan got to the core of my soul. I pounded on the shower wall over and over and over until I heard a loud clanging noise. I had no clothes on, and I could not let anybody find me out. I peered over the shower stall and saw someone in a cheerleading outfit fleeing. I could only hope they did not see me, and if they did, that they wouldn't tell. What was I going to do? How was I going to go on? Where would I find relief? Too many questions, no answers.

I had no problem waking up on Monday morning. I was so paranoid someone would come and find me staying in the school that I practically slept with one eye open. Thankfully, Sunday was really peaceful; nobody came around the school. I made sure that I did not do anything to set off any alarms. I might have lied to Coach Strong about my mom coming to pick me up, but I did not tell him a fib about watching film.

Our coaching staff had scouted the next three teams we were about to play. I had done my part checking them out. When I looked back over our film for the past couple of weeks, I did

see some plays that I missed. While I was not listening to every critique Coach Strong had for me during our film session, I could see where I needed work.

A lot of my teammates watched film all the time. I had taken for granted that I knew my position. I could clearly see just by watching myself and going back over the footage that I was getting better.

Maybe if I applied myself to my books, I could get better at that as well. Since Landon's dad was the preacher, Landon would often pick me up to go to church with him. He had called four times on Sunday. I did not want him to know where I was or what I was doing. My only problem was that I was hungry. Coach Strong had snacks all around because he was not the smallest man. My problem would be how I could replace those snacks before he realized someone had dipped their hand in his cookie jar and took some.

When you got to school, you could wait in the commons area to study, talk, dance, or anything sensible until it was time for the bell to ring. Then students could meander the hall-ways. I was always the last one there. My mom

worked a late shift, and when she got in, she'd bring me to school. When I rode the bus, I was there on time but never early. My teammates saw me sitting in the commons area and were surprised.

Landon came over to me and said, "You're here early. What's up? You can't return any-body's phone calls? You drop your phone in the toilet or something?"

"I wasn't feeling well yesterday. Can a brother get a break? Dang. I need to find you a girl and quick, because you bugging me like I'm your woman. Slow your roll, partner."

"Oh, it's like that?" Landon said.

I knew that I had embarrassed him a little. I did not mean to make him feel bad, but I needed him to back off. The best way to shut Landon up was to tease him a little bit. He backed off every time. He could dish it out, but he could not take it.

Blake came over and said, "Look, this thing with Shameek is heating up. Word has it he's planning to finish what he started a couple of weeks ago."

"He ain't gonna bring no gun to school," I said. "Plus, I got you. He talks all that junk, but

the police are just waiting for him to slip up so they can throw him in jail."

"Yeah, but I don't want to be a corpse and that be the reason why they go after Shameek. You know what I'm saying?" Blake lamented.

I always knew he was a little scaredy-cat. Coach Strong was tough, but his son was more of a pretty boy. He was cool people though. He was not selfish. It was not his fault that he was born with a silver spoon in his mouth. They call me *The Man* on defense, but as the quarterback, he was the true man on our team.

Shameek Elliot and I grew up together in the same hood. Our mamas used to be girls. Some kind of way, the Axes got control of him and had him swinging dope in school. He started selling back in middle school. He turned crazy. He tried to recruit me, but when my mom went to him saying she had already lost a husband and she did not want to lose her son, Shameek backed off.

I knew he and I would not have any problems. I just kept looking the other way. If dummies wanted to pay him for crack, then they were wack and deserved what they got.

However, when Shameek busted up a girl's face, and Blake had a lil' somethin' somethin' going on with that girl, he had a showdown with Shameek. I would not have said nothing if they went at it fist to fist and man to man. But Shameek did not want to play fair, and he pulled out steel on Blake. Like my last name, I pulled one back out on him. While I told Blake no worries, I had not been able to walk the streets without watching my back ever since.

Maybe it was not a bad thing that I could not live in my apartment anymore. I needed to keep a low profile for a number of reasons. Blake needed to do the same, but as the quarterback of our team, he was always in the spotlight so that was hard to do.

"There they go," Blake said. "Look, look at his hands. He's packing." Blake eyed Shameek suspiciously.

That was not the case. He was just scared. Shameek was not alone. He had about five deep with him. He was headed our direction.

"Blake, go on to class," I turned around and said. Then I turned to Landon and Brenton. "Y'all, take him away."

Shameek stepped to me and said, "What? You gonna have Blake Weak walk away from me?"

"It's Blake Strong."

"He ain't acting like it. But that's fine. I'll give you his butt whupping," Shameek said, stepping even closer.

I pushed him back. "Man, get off me."

"You wanted a fair fight. No iron, right?"

I said, "I don't want no fight at all."

"Oh, you gonna have something. You stepped in my way. Either you can step out of it or I'm going to have to permanently remove you. You ain't nothing but a punk anyway," he ranted and spit in my face.

It was on at that moment. What did I have to lose? I took my right hand and socked him.

"Wait a minute, school hasn't even started!" our principal, Dr. Sapp, yelled out. "What is going on here? You know what? I'm not having it."

Shameek threw his hands up. "Dr. Sapp, you saw it. I ain't have nothing to do with it."

Dr. Sapp said, "I see a whole bunch of brothers wearing light blue bandanas that they are not supposed to have in my school. That's what I see."

"Oh, so he gets off scot-free?" Shameek lobbied.

"Take the bandanas off and go on to class," Dr. Sapp said to Shameek and his thugs.

"You better be glad the principal is with you," Shameek taunted.

"Whatever, I'm here any time," I said. Dr. Sapp tugged my shirt and walked me to his office.

"Have you absolutely lost your mind? Are you crazy?"

"What, Dr. Sapp? What? They are in a gang and you do nothing."

"Don't try me, Leo."

"I'm just saying if you know they are in a gang, why do you let them stay in your school?"

"I got to catch them doing something and not catch other people doing something to them," he growled. "Now I got to punish you. You are supposed to be concentrating on x's and o's. You got a good thing going, man. Your grades came across my desk, and they already need work, and now you will have discipline problems. I know your mama is working hard to raise you the right way. Now I have to call her about this, and it ain't gonna be nice giving you suspension."

I realized he could not send me home. There was no home for me to go to. I had to get my free breakfast and lunch at the school.

"Come on, sir. I'm sorry, Dr. Sapp. I'm sorry, for real. We can make it to state."

"I have to keep my eye on you, Steele. I tell you what, I'm working in-school suspension this week; head on down there. Maybe if you're in there, you can concentrate more. There's one kid already in there."

And that kid would not stop talking. Thankfully, the day flew by because he ran his mouth so much. Then ISS got interesting when one of the cheerleaders, Ella Blount, walked in. She was a twin, and the way she looked at me, it was as if she knew I was staying at the school. Was she the one who saw me in the shower? If so, it was just my doggone luck. As my dad used to say, if it weren't for bad luck, I'd have no luck at all. However, since adversity builds character, I would have to keep pressing and move on.

CHAPTER 2
Truly Saved

So, Leo, where do you live?" Ella asked me in ISS when we had our lunch break.

I could not stop staring at the hamburger on her plate. I gobbled mine up so fast. It was hard not having any dinner to eat.

"Did you hear me? Hello!" she repeated.

Ella was a really cute girl. Beautiful teeth, precious smile, curves that went on for days, and unlike her sister, Eva, I probably didn't notice her because Ella never flaunted what she had. However, being locked in a small room with her, I could not help but notice she was extremely attractive.

When she kept asking me nosy questions, I got irritated. "Aren't we supposed to be concentrating on our work?"

"It's lunch time, dude," the other person in ISS said to me.

It was this guy named Carlen. He was in the eleventh grade also, but he did not roll in the circles Ella and I shared. He was interesting, to say the least. He was flaming and proud of it. He did not make me uncomfortable, but I did not like a know-it-all.

"I'm sorry. I didn't know asking you where you lived was a touchy subject," Ella replied.

"You know where I live," I responded. She had been to parties around my way.

We'd known of each other since middle school. We hung out with the same folks. I knew Ella kept looking at me, studying me, reading me, and questioning me because she was definitely the one who saw me Saturday in the locker room. As I thought back to more than what was going on in my own world, I remembered when I was in the parking lot talking to my mom that the cheerleaders were assembling for some trip.

Two of my defensive teammates, Amir and Brenton, were dating two of the cheerleaders. Watching film, they had been talking about going to see them perform at a competition, so it made sense.

It *was* Ella. Knowing Eva like I did, because I had more classes with Eva over the years, she would have just come out and asked me. Ella was not shy, but she was not rude or brash either. She was trying to beat around the bush to get out the information she wanted. Obviously she cared, because she kept looking and seemed to want to make sure I was okay. I could not risk confirming her suspicions until I found somewhere else to go.

Broaching the subject gingerly, Ella said, "I don't really feel good. I'm not going to eat all this. Don't want to waste it. Either of you guys want it?"

Carlen's little skinny self said, "Nah, I'm watching my figure. You ought to understand that, girlfriend."

"How 'bout you, Leo?" Ella offered.

When I saw her cut her burger in half and not eat her fries, I let my pride go. I guess I was

salivating. I was hungry, but I could not appear too pitiful.

"If you are not gonna eat it."

"Boy, you better take that food. And quit looking at her like you wanna gobble her up with the plate. I'm just as fine," Carlen teasingly sulked.

I did not even want to play with him. Carlen was a cool guy. Word was out he helped a few people dress for the prom last year. However, I did not swing that way, and I had enough friends. I did not want to send wrong messages. After lunch I went back over to my little corner and stared at my work.

The next day was more of the same. The three of us in ISS were buried under piles of paper. Dr. Sapp sat at the front desk and lectured.

Our principal said, "You know when students make dumb choices, they land themselves in here. I hope they get it and understand fighting, stealing, and cheating will lead them down the wrong path that they may never recover from. I've always told you guys, I used to cut up in school. So I understand you may want to make a little extra money, so you steal. Or you don't

want your manhood threatened, so you fight. Or you don't want to let down friends, so you cheat. Stealing, fighting and cheating are stupid. Matter of fact, I want you all to write me a paper about why what you did was dumb. Persuade me that you'll never do it again."

"But, Dr. Sapp! C'mon, man, you see all these papers and work we gotta do. Cut us a break, sir," Carlen lobbied.

Dr. Sapp said, "Don't try to change my mind. I need you all to learn that what you did was wrong. I'm going out to the hallway. Get to it."

I could not believe Ella had cheated. I had heard about her sister, Eva, selling the answers to the US History test for five dollars. Knowing that I needed to pull up my grade in that class, I probably would have paid. I thought Eva was getting the answers from the teacher's desk, not from her sister. Even if that was the case, Ella was not the mastermind behind it all. Why was she the one who ended up in here? However, of all people, I understood that family was a trip.

When Carlen went to the restroom and it was just Ella and me in ISS, I said, "You should not let anybody use you."

"You shouldn't let anybody provoke you to fight," she snapped back.

"Yeah, but I hit somebody who deserved it. If people don't study, they don't deserve to get the answers. Or were you getting some of the money from the sale?" I asked. Ella looked at me and gritted her teeth.

I could tell her answer was no. She probably had no idea what her sister was even doing. That was crazy to me.

"I'm not trying to get in your business," I said, making sure I didn't give her a door to walk into my world. "I'm just saying once things happen, you can really see who has your back and who doesn't. You can't pick your family, but you surely can pick whether you let them use you or not. And you just shouldn't let anybody walk over you; that's all."

I did not mean to make her tear up, but obviously what I was saying cut close to her heart. I could not have imagined what it was like having a twin, but if I had one, they would be the last person I would think who would sell me out.

For some reason I had a mental block when it came to doing my work. I did not know if it

was that I could not understand the material in the first place or if a couple of days with no dinner was taking its toll on me. Either way, when Dr. Sapp came in and demanded our work, I looked stupid not having it. I did not want more days extended to my stay in ISS. I certainly did not want him to suspend me. I could have kicked myself for not maximizing my time. He was a calm guy; it took a lot to ruffle him, but everyone had their limits. I did not know if he would go for days spent in ISS without any work being done.

After Ella and Carlen turned in their assignments, he looked at me. I stared back. He glared harder, like I needed to produce something or I would not like the consequences.

"What's going on, Steele? You want to play the rest of the season? I need to see some work. What's up?"

"We did ours together," Ella cut in.

Dr. Sapp looked at her in a strange way. Ella wasn't backing down. I knew I did not work with her. She knew I did not work with her, but there she was, helping me anyway. I was shocked she would save me like that.

"We have the same classes," Ella said with a matter-of-fact tone. "I know why it's such a surprise. You weren't in here a lot, so you didn't see us working together. You told us to get it done. You didn't say we couldn't work together. Since there were things both of us helped each other with, we just did it together. So there you go."

"His name is not on this paper." Dr. Sapp tried catching her.

"My name isn't either," she replied.

"Why is it all in your handwriting?" he asked.

" 'Cause I write better than him."

"Carlen, is this true?" Dr. Sapp asked.

"Yes, sir," Carlen agreed with a wink my way when Dr. Sapp looked at the papers.

I had too much pride built up in me to tell Ella thank you. All I had been going through for the last couple of days, I surely did need help. She came through for me and that meant a lot.

At the end of the day, I thought the coaches would never leave. We had an important season; they wanted to be prepared. However, they were going all out. It was nine, and I was tired.

Also, I had another problem. Landon was getting very suspicious because he used to drive me home. For the last two days when he asked if I was ready, I made up something that even I did not believe.

Thankfully, I had my shower out of the way. When I came off the field, I immediately got in the shower. Coach had already fussed at the team for not putting the towels up to get washed. I realized it was me because as soon as everyone took showers, the managers loaded up the washing machine. The washer was so high-tech I did not know how to use it, and to wash one towel did not make sense. I also had not figured out how to eat when there was no food around. I was starving. My stomach was growling. Coach had removed his snacks since he thought other coaches were stealing them, and there was absolutely nothing to grub on laying around.

I was a little paranoid being in the school alone. I heard squealing. I made sure I got my foot off the floor thinking that rats crawled around at night. Then I heard a different noise, and I got up to investigate. Pebbles were hitting the window in Coach's office. I went over to the

window, lifted up the blind, and saw a taped-up note with an arrow pointing down.

If I were a little child, I would have thought an elf helped Santa bring just the right thing for Christmas. It was like a holiday. I bypassed the alarm, put a brick in the door, ran outside, and grabbed the fluorescent pink wicker basket covered with a kitchen towel.

I looked around to see if I could find anybody, but I did not see a soul. When I got inside, it took me no time to tear into the fried chicken, collard greens, macaroni and cheese, and cornbread. The delicious meal saved me.

The next day in ISS, I did not want to be so near Ella. I did not want to put her on the spot. I wanted to tell her that I knew what she was doing, but I also did not want to be embarrassed.

When she went to the restroom, Carlen said, "It doesn't take a lot of smarts to figure out the girl likes you. First I was jealous 'cause I wanted you to have eyes for me, but as slowly as you move, I'm glad you are looking at her too. If you don't intervene, I got time to turn straight and put the moves on her myself."

"I'm not trying to get a girlfriend right now," I said, trying not to laugh at his joke.

"Oh yeah, you just stare at her half the day."

"I was trying to steal something out of her purse, but every time I want to go for it, I catch you looking dead over in her direction. See, I got jokes too," I said to Carlen.

"Yeah, I learned my lesson for trying to get my hustle on. But I'm just saying, man, if you gonna look that hard, try to touch."

"Whatever."

"I got your 'whatever,'" Carlen said, wanting to make me own up to the feeling I could not deny.

I figured I was going to be ready for Ella later in the evening. I suspected that she was going to bring me a basket of food. While it could have been a baloney sandwich or just two pieces of bread, I was ready to eat. I knew she was not going to let me down. My plan was to go out there and thank her. Sure enough, around nine there was a knock on Coach's window. I did not even have to go and see what it was. I immediately

went outside. I saw Ella fly around the corner. I was about to follow her, but my attention was grabbed as three cars came speeding into the school parking lot. As the cars appeared to be racing uncontrollably, I froze.

Everybody knew the Axes had initiation every fall. If you were driving and saw a carload of teens going really slow, you shouldn't beep at them because they might shoot you. If you were a girl, you shouldn't walk alone because they might rape you. If you had issues with them, you shouldn't get in their way because they might kill you. However, I didn't see Ella get in a car, and I had to stay out there to make sure she was safe.

After the race, Shameek got out of the winning car. He was screaming and yelling that he was the man. I was not even in their little group, and I knew they let him win since he was their so-called leader.

Where was Ella? Certainly she did not walk here. I did not think she had a car, but I did not see another car leave. Again, I had to make sure she was okay now that Shameek had won. I was just waiting for him to get back in his car.

Hopefully, Ella noticed that they were out there too and stayed hidden.

Problem was, Shameek didn't leave. He and his crew pulled out spray cans from the trunks of their cars and started painting on the school bricks. Without even thinking of the consequences, I yelled out.

"Who's there?" Shameek's sidekick, a thug named Bruno, called out.

I did not want to lead them toward the door because if they found out how to get into the place, it would be trashed.

Hoping Shameek would not try to show out, I walked toward him and said, "It's Leo, just waiting on my ride."

"What? It's Steele! Must be my lucky night," Shameek taunted.

"I don't want no trouble with you, Shameek," I said. "My mom will be here any minute."

"Oh, I got boys right here who would love to meet your pretty mom. As a matter of fact, we been looking at your crib, but ain't nobody came to your place. You scared of me?"

I took a few steps closer. I did not want to antagonize him; however, I was not a punk. So

when he kept talking about my mama, I shut him up by giving him two upper cuts. Problem was, I was outnumbered. It was just me and about eleven of them. Kicks, punches, jabs, hits, and licks came from all directions.

I didn't know how long the beating went on. I do believe, however, that if the sirens I vaguely heard had not come screaming into the parking lot, the gang would have stuck around and beaten me to a pulp. In all the mayhem, I passed out.

"Do I hear crying? Is that a female voice? Is my mom here?" I wondered, trying to open my eyes.

When I did try to see, it was painful and blurry. As I reached up to touch my face, I could tell it was swollen. I also saw I was in a gown in a hospital room. Ella was standing over me, turning to leave. Just as she was about to walk away, I touched her arm.

"Stay, please."

She paused and a few tears fell. "Oh, Leo, this is horrible. I couldn't let them do this to you."

Now it was coming back to me. I had taken a few pain pills that the nurse had given me; therefore, I was a little out of it. Whatever Ella was saying, I did not fully understand. Clearly, I could see she cared. It totally surprised me. I was trying to tell her that I cared too. I was out there because I did not want anything to happen to her in that parking lot.

"I'm not supposed to be in here. Amir and Hallie distracted the nurse, and I snuck in. I just wanted to make sure you were going to be okay. You are gonna be okay, right?" she asked. She leaned down by me and gently stroked my brow.

Though the touch of her skin felt really good, I cringed because any movement to my bruised face hurt. Of course, I tried to be tough. Ella had to know I was not a wimp.

"Give me your mom's number, and I'll call her. I will be sure to tell her you are okay. It would not be great for a parent to get a phone call that their kid is in the emergency room," Ella stated.

I turned away. That's when I realized I really needed to get out of the hospital. I could not talk to the police about why I was at the school.

Then I got frightened because the gym door was still propped open.

"Okay. Thanks for coming. I don't feel good," I responded to Ella, hoping she got the point to leave. I didn't want her to go. She could have stayed all night making sure I was okay, but spending time with her would have to wait. I had to figure out a plan. Just as she had snuck in, I was going to have to sneak out.

I was not feeling one hundred percent. However, I was football player. I could take a little pounding. Shameek and his thugs were not going to be able to hold me down.

"If you need anything, call me," Ella said.

"Are my clothes over there?"

"You don't need any clothes. You just need to rest."

"No, I was going to tell you to put your phone number in my phone," I replied, thinking quickly, because as soon as she was gone I needed to go too.

Ella found my phone and put in her number. Watching her leave, I knew I definitely had to do what Carlen said. It was time I stepped up and let her know how much I appreciated

her. Every day she was doing something amazing for me.

I was struggling to get dressed. I realized I had a bruised chest. My ribs weren't sore, but someone must have given me a good whack right in the center of my breastbone.

"Uh, where do you think you're going?" Coach Strong said as he came in the room. "We need to talk, Leo, and I need the truth."

At that moment I laid back down on the bed. I needed a big break. It was not good.

"Son, sit up. I need you to talk to me," Coach said. "Where have you been staying?"

"Coach, I got it under control."

"That is not an answer to my question, Steele, and you know it. I think you lied to me, young man. Of all the young men in my program, you've always owned up to your stuff. Saturday, when you asked to stay after to watch film, you said your mom was going to get you. Was that the truth?"

He got no response. I felt bad that I had lied to him. I had no choice now but to come clean. He knew something was up. The best thing I had going for me was being on his football team.

I had to come clean so I would not lose that. I turned toward him with tears in my eyes.

Completely vulnerable, I said, "My mom came to the school earlier to tell me good-bye. She moved to New York. Basically, told me I gotta find a way to make it on my own. She gave me a few dollars and was out."

"Why didn't you tell me, son? We could have figured something out."

"Tell you what, Coach? You're going through so much yourself. Your wife was just diagnosed with cancer. You are knee-deep in trying to win the state title. You don't have time to baby-sit me. So I stayed in your office."

"You've been the one eating all my food, huh? I should have known something else was going on. You clean up my office a lil' bit nicer than I leave it," he joked.

Where was this conversation going? Why was he softening when I thought he should be biting my head off? Was he serious when he said I should have told him? Would he have helped me?

"I was outside and saw trouble when I went to thank a cheerleader for bringing me food," I said, getting back to why things had escalated.

Going into "parent mode," Coach Strong asked, "You haven't been eating, son?"

"When you took away the snacks? No, sir, not at night. My only meals were during breakfast and lunch."

Shaking his head, he got back to the big blow up. "So you went out to get the food; that's when you saw the guys?"

"Yeah, I wanted to make sure they wouldn't hurt her. And I didn't know where she went. So I stayed out there. They were drag racing. Next thing I knew, they were spray painting on the school property. You taught us, Coach, to stand for stuff. I knew if they saw me go into the school, they'd try to get in too."

"And they would tear it up," Coach said, completely feeling me.

"Exactly, so I paid the price."

"Leo, you saved the building," Coach declared with pride.

"But now that you know, I have nowhere to go, Coach. My mom says I'm eighteen, and I can make it on my own. I ain't got nowhere to go, Coach. What am I gonna do? Please, don't throw me off the team, Coach. I'm sorry I lied."

"Don't worry about that. Just rest up so you can be able to play."

"These lil' nicks can't get me down, Coach. Please, don't throw me off the team."

He paced around the room. He put his hands on his hips, and then he sat down in the chair on the other side of the room. I didn't know if he was thinking, praying, or screaming in his head. Finally, he said, "You are gonna come stay with me and my family."

When I heard that, I could have gone out and made three sacks for him! He words encouraged me. I was truly saved.

CHAPTER 3
Be Still

Coach, are you serious? You don't mind me staying with you guys?" I asked. I was completely overwhelmed at the thought of him being so generous. What a relief!

"It shouldn't be a problem because you're eighteen, right?" Coach asked, ignoring the fact that I was a little emotional about his decision. "I'm gonna step out to get the nurse and see if she can get your mom on the phone."

When Coach left, I leaned over and looked at my phone. The last number in there was Ella's. I desperately wanted to call her and make sure she was safe. I also wanted to thank her for so much, but instead I called my mother.

"Yeah, boy, what's up?" the gruff male voice answered.

I knew it was Frankie. His yucky tone told me he knew it was me. I wondered why he answered her phone. He knew I was not calling to speak with him.

"Is my mom there?"

"You can't say hello?" he taunted.

"Frankie, let's not pretend we're cool, man. I'm just trying to speak to my mom."

"She's busy right now, partner. She's going to have to call you back tomorrow or next week or something. Just because she left you this phone doesn't mean you have to wear it out. We're trying to get acquainted with one another, you know."

"Frankie, I'm not asking you if I can speak to my mom. I'm telling you I need to speak to her. I'm in the hospital."

"Dang, I always knew you were a trouble-maker. Hold on."

I wanted to go through the cell phone and strangle him. Since he always thought I was in trouble, I needed to go to jail for whupping his tail. Why was she with him?

My mom frantically got on the phone and said, "Leo, you're in jail?"

"Mom, no, the hospital. I just got into a little fight. It's not that big. I'm sure the doctors want to know about insurance and stuff."

"Leo, you got a medical card. It should be in your wallet. It says AmeriTech on it."

"Oh, I thought that was the dental card."

"Yeah, it's both. If you give that to them, then you'll be okay. Are you okay?"

"I'm fine, Mom. I just wish you were here."

"I wish I was too, baby."

"Why'd you have to go, Mom?"

"Where are you staying?" she asked me a question instead of answering mine.

"You left me no choice really, Ma. I was staying at the school."

"What?"

"Now Coach Strong wants me to stay with him, but I think he wants to talk to you first."

"He's gonna think I'm horrible."

"Ya think?" I wanted to tell her. She needed to be here. New York might have the job, but it did not have her son. Why were her priorities so messed up?

"You're just gonna have to explain that I had to try this up here."

She stopped talking. I could sense in her voice that things were not going just the way she wanted them to. It had only been a couple days, so I did not press her. I knew she made the wrong decision. Frankie was a jerk no matter what she thought. He could rub all up on her legs and make her think all was good with the world, but even when a snake sheds its skin, it was still a snake. He was a jerk here, and he would still be a jerk in New York.

"Can you just tell Coach Strong that for me?"

"Mom, he wants to talk to you."

And as if on cue, he walked back into my room. The nurse was with him and had begun to check me out. I handed Coach the phone.

After a few minutes Coach said, "Well, all right, Mrs. Steele, Leo will be at my place. Let me give you my home number. He's got a pretty good gash on the side of his head."

A lady from hospital administration came in. I had to sign a few papers and give them my insurance card. Before Coach Strong hung up the phone, he gave it back to me.

"Baby, I do love you," my mom said, sounding like she was trying to convince herself. "Take care and don't get into trouble, okay?"

When we hung up the phone, Coach Strong said, "I just finished talking to someone from the Department of Children and Family Services. Since you are eighteen, you are able to come and stay with me. You're mom says it's okay too, so let's get you home. I've got a guest room you can stay in. Blake will be thrilled to have you there."

I have been in front of Blake's house many times, but I've never been inside. All of us were scared that Coach would get on to us about something. It looked really nice on the outside, but boy, it was really something special inside. Blake had it made. He was the first one I saw when I got there.

"What's up, Steele?" he said. We gave each other dap.

When I looked up and he saw my face, he said, "Ouch, man. Dang!"

He did not even have to ask who did it. The look that I had in my eyes told him that his greatest fears of the Axes striking out at the two of us were realized.

"You know you can't hide here because they'll find me too. Tell me you didn't tell my dad that I was involved with all of this. He doesn't know Shameek and the Axes came at you because I came at them, does he?"

I shook my head as Coach Strong came by and said, "Blake, take Leo to the guest bedroom."

"I'll show him around, Dad," Blake's younger sister, Lola, said. She was in the seventh grade, and she was prancing to the door like the hostess with the mostest.

Lola took me by the hand and led me down the hall. I looked back at Blake, and he looked upset. To be honest, I could not figure out why he was acting that way. I stuck my neck in his business so he would not get a bullet in any part of his body. Now, when I needed him to rescue me, he wanted me far away. He was not the only one upset at that point.

My phone started ringing. I had it a little too loud, and I did not want it to disturb the Strongs. Quickly, I picked it up.

Responding like a friend, Landon yelled, "Man, you all right? You in the hospital? I'm on my way. Where you at?"

"I'm good, and I'm not in the hospital any-more," I said. "How'd you find out?"

"Brenton called me and said Amir told him that you got rushed to the hospital. Word's out you've been staying at the school. Is that true, man?"

"Look, I don't want everyone in my busi-ness," I said in a defensive tone.

"I'm just saying, man, you know I'm your brother. You could've stayed here with me. It ain't even like my parents would know or that they would have had a problem with it."

"You might be right, but the Axes are trip-ping, and I didn't want to put a lead on your trail."

"Oh, so you think being out there by yourself is the way to go?"

"I'm all right."

"Today," Landon emphasized. "We're just gonna have to come up with a plan. I'll talk to Blake—"

Cutting Landon off, I said, "Blake? Please, that punk ain't gonna do nothing. He's just wor-ried about his own self."

"Well, y'all gonna have to stick together be-cause it's both of y'all who they're after."

"How you seem to know so much about the Axes and what they want to do anyway?" Leo questioned. "You know they all on my jock. You don't even need to be talking to them, Landon. They don't know how to take no for an answer."

The phone got silent. I knew he was taking in what I said. Why he wanted to be accepted at any cost was beyond me.

I scolded, "Think about what I said. We'll talk about this later. I'm going to bed."

"Okay, see you tomorrow, Mom," Landon joked. "For real, glad you're all right though, Le."

"Right, right."

Coach Strong told me to make myself at home. I was a little hungry. I felt so uncomfortable about going in their refrigerator, but I was starving. I had some pain pills that I needed water to take down. Thankfully, there was a light on in the kitchen. I was happy that Coach was probably in there. As I got closer, I heard a conversation that paralyzed me.

"Bradley, I don't know if bringing this boy into our home is good. Getting into fights with a gang? Obviously, things are not over if the boys fled the scene. You have a teenage son who's

already a handful to raise. I just don't know if this is a good idea," Mrs. Strong said.

"I understand, honey, and I know we got a lot going on. I'm sorry to stress you. But of all the young men on my team, Leo's had the roughest time. He's tough, but he's also a teddy bear. He'd give his right arm for you if you needed it. I didn't know he was staying at the school and not eating. He needs somebody right now, and I just can't turn my back. Please, baby, please say you're okay with this."

His wife did not respond, but they hugged. I thought it was interesting how they dealt with conflict. It certainly hurt that she did not want me here. I knew I was going to have to find somewhere else to stay to get out of her way. Until then, I just would not do anything to cause any problems.

"Oh, so everything Leo did for you, you forgot about? You gotta give him attitude when he comes to your house to live," Landon went off on Blake. A group of football players stood around in the atrium, waiting for the bell to allow us to go to class.

Blake looked over at me, like I sold him out by talking too much. I just shrugged my shoulders and turned the other way. I did not ask Landon to confront Blake. I certainly was not expecting Blake to be a jerk about me staying at his place. Whatever backlash he got from some of our teammates was on him. I had wound up in a big mess defending Blake, and I sure was not going to do it again. Plus, I had doubts that Blake even appreciated my help.

"Step back, Landon. Get on out of my face," Blake said, trying to walk away.

"Nah, nah, we're going to deal with this," Landon said. "The Axes left him for dead Wednesday night because of your tail."

Blake shot me a sympathetic look this time. It was so late when we came in, his dad only gave him the basics of why I was staying. He did not tell him what happened to me. I did not want the world to know, but Amir told Brenton, and Brenton told Landon, which was why Landon called me. And if Landon knew, the whole school knew.

Brenton came over and said, "Leo, why are you even here today?"

"I spent all day yesterday in the Strong's guest room. This is the last day of ISS. It's just some bruises and a little gash with some stitches that'll dissolve on their own. I'm all right. We're defensive brothers. Come on, Brenton. You'd laugh at me if I stayed home because of a few cuts."

"Right, right," he said, giving me five. He still looked at me like I was crazy for coming to school after such a beating.

Landon continued yelling at Blake. "You so doggone selfish, man. We play so hard behind you, but if anybody else has a good game or a good practice and gets compliments from your dad, then you just don't want to have nothing to do with them. You think you're the only reason why we're 3–0?"

Blake did not respond. Landon took two of his fingers and poked Blake in the chest. Blake shook his head like he was about to tackle Landon. The guys stepped in the way.

"Nah, y'all get out the way. Apparently, we need to do this. I'm tired of Blake Strong thinking he's all that," Landon yelled.

"What's your skinny behind going to do?" Blake yelled back at the lean, tall receiver who didn't have much meat on his bones but could fly.

Landon had been balling lately. He was doing his thing at practice, catching balls that Blake had thrown off course and gaining many yards after the catch. So focused on my own world, I did not even put two and two together. Blake was tripping when his dad gave Landon compliments. More shoving kept going on. Brenton held Blake and Amir held Landon, but a crowd was starting to gather.

Finally, I stepped in the middle of all of it and said, "Look, I got one more day in ISS, and I ain't trying to have y'all join me. If y'all come in there, Dr. Sapp might give me more time just because." I looked at Landon. "Go to class."

"I'm trying to help you. Doc, what's up?" Landon vented.

I whispered, "I ain't ask you, man. At least for now, I have to live with that cat."

Landon scolded, "No, you don't. You can come stay with me."

"Thanks, man."

We slapped hands. "Real love, man," Landon affirmed.

"Real love," I responded back.

I went on to class, but Blake walked up beside me and said, "Look, if you think I was wrong to not be overly hospitable, I apologize. You didn't have to go and tell Landon and get him all jacked about the situation. Last thing we want is our team divided."

"Blake, if you're going to apologize, that's on you. You don't have to. I don't want to be at your house no longer than you want me to be there. Even though the room I'm staying in is clear across the other side of the house, it ain't like you gotta see me tripping for real. Landon was right for calling you out. Shameek could have shot you a long time ago. I stopped that, and now my life is practically over with me being homeless and all, and you don't wanna put yourself out to help me. What's up? It ain't like your mama gonna wanna tuck me in bed at night. I ain't trying to take your place."

Blake tried explaining, "We just have a lot going on at my house right now."

"I know that, and I'm not trying to do anything to cause problems."

"But you are causing problems. It's not right to be upset by the fact that you're there, okay? I can't explain it."

Angry at his selfishness, I said, "Well, deal with it. It's not my job to make you comfortable."

Restraining from socking him, I walked to ISS. Blake had some nerve. He needed to realize we were on the same team. He could not be so uptight.

"Why are you here, Leo?" Ella said when I walked into the room.

"I'm doing okay, plus I wanted to see you," I declared, not holding back with her any more.

Then, of course, Dr. Sapp came into the room and gave us one of his daily lectures, "Okay, so it's just you two today. Carlen is done with his time in ISS and he's out. I hope you guys learn something. It's your last day, and I don't want to have to see you guys any more."

"We've caught up on our entire work, sir."

"Well, you help him study today," Dr. Sapp said to Ella. "I just want to tell you guys that you don't always get second chances in this life. You two are juniors in high school. Before you know it, you'll be out on your own making your mark

in society. You mess up out there … you don't get do overs. I know making dumb decisions is a part of growing up; consider yourselves experienced. Miss Ella, I hope you learned that standing up for people isn't always worth it. Helping people cheat by saying they assisted you with an assignment when they didn't is wrong.

I looked at Ella. She looked at me. We both knew we were busted about the work she said I'd done with her.

He continued, "Yeah, don't look at me like that. I know he didn't help you. If you want to help your peers, your sister, or some guy you think is cool, then really equip them to stand on their own two feet. And, Mr. Steele?"

"Yes, sir," I said.

"Come here. Let me see you in the hallway."

Ella looked at me like, *Ooh, you are in trouble*. She sort of chuckled and her smile was beautiful.

When I stepped out into the hallway with Dr. Sapp, he said, "I told you messing with them Axes is crazy. You know I know what happened up here."

"You gonna press charges on me, sir?"

"Nah, the school house is supposed to be a lot of things to people. It's not meant to be your home, but occasionally that's all we got. The little beat down you got ... I guess that's enough punishment."

"Ha-ha-ha, sir."

"I was just like you when I was young. I had a lot of potential, but I got a little off track because of my circumstances. I'm just telling you, I don't want you trying to exact revenge. When people show you they are crazy, believe them. If you see them in the halls, go the other way. Trust me, I'm trying everything to get their tails out of my school for good. Until that happens, you know you're at the top of their list. So just lay low. You got me?"

"Yes, sir."

"I'm going to go walk the halls and make sure everyone's where they are supposed to be. Let the girl help you with some school work. She's very smart, and I've seen the way you've been checking her out. Don't just try to get in her pants. You better try to get in her mind."

"Dr. Sapp, come on, man," I cried, completely embarrassed.

"Don't play with me. I was young. I'm still a man. I'm single and I know. However, get this; I didn't become the principal of this large high school without knowledge. Knowledge is money, partner. You wanna go somewhere, you wanna be someone, then like the song says in *Sister Act 2*, you better wake up and pay attention."

I replied, "I have never seen *Sister Act 2*."

"Oh, well, that's what y'all gonna watch today. Be right back," he smiled and was gone.

I hated musicals, but maybe it could teach me something I did not know. Maybe … maybe not.

On Saturday, Coach wanted us to give back. We were hosting a football clinic for kids ages eight and under. There would be about one hundred or so little rug rats running around, and I would be in football hell.

As I recalled from the last time we gave back, some of those kids were real young. When you told them to run right, they ran left. You could not stand directly in front of them and show them drills because their coordination was not there yet. It was sweet, but I sure did not

want to get out of the plush bed for that. I was relaxing when Coach got me and Blake up.

There were several stations, but I was a floater. Coach had me walking around making sure everything was going smoothly. When I got over to a group of kids who were teasing this one very little boy, I went off. I did not like anyone bullying anybody. I wanted to take the bad kids, put them over my knee, and spank them hard. Instead, I took the little boy who was targeted over to the side and calmed him down. He was okay, so I started teaching him drills.

"I got it. I know it," the little man said after we played for about ten minutes.

"Tell me your name," I said to him.

"I'm Evan."

"Hey, Evan. I'm Leo. Evan, you can be a good football player. We're going to play a little scrimmage game in a minute, and you're going to get a touchdown, okay?"

I held out my hand, and he gave me a high-five. He was the cutest little joker. He had such spunk. Now he had confidence, and he was going to whup up on those guys who dissed him.

"You did a really good job with him, young man," this guy said to me over my shoulder.

I turned around. The stranger was holding out his hand. I shook it.

"Daddy, watch me get a touchdown," Evan screamed with excitement to the man.

"Oh, this is your son," I said, not realizing the boy's father was around watching. "Go run the long route, Evan."

I put the ball in the little guy's hands. He tucked it under. Little Evan ran all over the boys who had taunted him.

The gentleman said, "You're impressive. What grade are you in?"

"I'm a junior."

"Well, I'm an NFL agent. I'll be watching you. What kind of grades do you have?"

It was a normal question. However, the words got to me. Thankfully, I did not have to answer when Evan ran back with Ella.

"Hey," I said to her.

"Hey," Evan's father greeted Ella in a friendly tone like he knew her or something.

She had a weird look on her face. It was like everybody knew something but me. I was left out

of the joke. Come to find out Evan was her little brother and this was her dad. Then I got really nervous. I had been with many girls. A brother did his thing. However, this was the first time I ever let one in. She did not even know that I had feelings for her, and being around her father made my palms sweat.

Ella sang my praises. Her dad was happy to know we were friends. I liked her even more at that point.

The next week flew by. I wanted to ask her out, but Coach Strong had us on a tight regimen. Staying with him, he knew my every move. Yeah, I could have called her at night, but it was so late. I did not want to bother her. While I had thought that Blake did not have to see me, we actually did everything together. We ate breakfast together. We ate dinner together. We had football practice together, and we had to study together. I was not in his way, but I was in his space.

I could not wait until Friday night. It was an away game. I was ready to show I could ball and get my aggression out the right way.

Brenton, Amir, and I had the defense jacked up. Our kicking game was the weakest. There were not many black kickers in the NFL or in D1 colleges, and it seemed as though that was probably a good thing because if they played like the one we had, then they would be poop. Now I knew brothers could do anything they wanted to, but for some reason kicking was not our thing. We wanted the hard-hitting jobs or the flashy positions. Kicking the ball through the uprights was a lot of pressure, but it was satisfying when executed well.

Knowing that our kicker was bad, we knew we really could not count on special teams. Offense and defense were going to have to show up. But Blake didn't adhere to the plan. He threw two picks on our offensive possessions. He seemed rattled. We knew defense had to win the game. Therefore, I got a forced fumble and gave the ball back to offense on the other team's ten yard line. We still could not score. Our kicker came out and could not get us three points.

While warming up to go back out on defense, Brenton said, "I hope ER gets eligible soon."

"Who's ER?" I asked.

"The new guy ... you know who he is. His dad is working on his eligibility," Brenton explained, though I still looked clueless.

"The white kid? Sheesh, you really did bump your head to miss him," Amir said, pointing to the guy standing with our kicker, trying to give him pointers.

I asked, "Is he good?"

"Yeah, he made a bunch at practice from the fifty yard line," Brenton said.

"And he's better than what we got," Amir remarked.

"True that, true that, but let's go win this game because he isn't playing now, and we're on a mission."

Three quarters later, we trounced the sorriest team in our division, 56–0, thanks to our defense scoring. On the bus ride back, normally the football players had to sit together, but since we won, Coach was more lenient. Some of the guys were paired up with cheerleaders and band girls.

I went over to Ella and said, "Is this seat taken?"

She batted her long eyelashes at me and said, "No."

She went to sleep on my shoulder. There was so much I wanted to say to her. She needed to know I cared and that I was not oblivious to all the great things she had done to help me. I wanted to tell her that, truthfully, if it was not for her coming to my rescue, who'd know where I'd be. However, she did not give me the chance because she started snoring. Though it was just a little, I knew she was in too deep of a sleep to be bothered.

"Nudge her," her sister said. "I don't want her embarrassing me by snoring on this bus."

Feeling protective, I said, "I got her. She's cool. She ain't bothering anybody on this bus. We all gonna be snoring in a minute."

Eva squinted at me. I knew she wanted to ask me if I liked her sister, but she did not say anything. Then she rolled her eyes. I did not care. I was already a little salty with her for leaving Ella out to dry with the whole cheating thing.

Actually, I dared anyone to say Ella was bothering them by snoring. It was the least I

could do, sticking up for her when she stuck up for me. When we got to the school, she was drooling a bit. I could tell she was a little embarrassed. I wanted to wipe her mouth, tell her it was okay, and give her a hug or a kiss or something, but I chickened out. Besides, I did not have any time to think when Coach Strong made sure Blake and I got in his car so we could head home.

I wanted him to stop bragging on me and saying I had such a good defensive game because I could tell it was getting under Blake's skin. It was night time, but it was light enough for me to tell that my brother was turning red. His father kept on pushing the issue. Blake was huffing.

To make matters worse, as soon as we got inside the house, Mrs. Strong rushed up to me and said, "I'm missing some money, Leo. It was just forty dollars, but now it's gone. I know you might need it for something, and you might have already spent it, but I would at least like you to admit you took it."

I looked over at Blake. He was snickering. He was enjoying that I was getting accused of something I did not do. This was a bunch of crap.

Coach Strong defended and said, "Why are you accusing him? There are other kids in this house, and you know I always need cash."

"Blake and Lola don't have to steal. So, Bradley, did you take it?" Mrs. Strong interrogated. "I didn't think so."

The two of them argued. Lola came out of her room, tearing up. Blake looked like he wanted to sock me.

So she would not stress herself out and get the cancer going in the wrong direction, I said, "I took it. I'm sorry."

I made my move. At that point I knew I had to accept the consequences. The two of them just kept on looking at each other not knowing what to do. I could tell Coach Strong really did not believe I had done it. The way I said it, his wife did not know if I was telling the truth. Not knowing what to do, I realized I'd better be still.

CHAPTER 4

Too Much

The entire weekend at the Strong's house was excruciating. Friday night after I confessed to taking the money, the Strongs didn't reprimand me. They just went their separate ways and practically avoided each other and me. As much as I could, I stayed in the guest room. I was still a little weak from my injuries. Plus with the intensity I gave on the football field, I needed to have some quiet.

Though Mrs. Strong's food was not as good as the baskets Ella brought, everything was pretty good. I was just thankful to be eating. I did not have to worry where my next meal was coming from.

Coach Strong wasn't even speaking to me. I knew that was bad, not so much because he thought I was trouble, but he was on eggshells because I was causing him trouble. Not wanting to be a bother, I got on the Internet and looked up rooms I could rent. Quickly, I got depressed because even though I found some in our district, I still didn't have a job.

Searching other places online, I ended up checking my grades. They were horrendous. I knew that something needed to be done about them before I got kicked off the team.

I called up Landon and said, "Wassup, guy? You going to that tutoring thing at the school?"

"I wasn't, but, uh, I could. I need to go to the mall, though, and pick up a few things. You ain't hanging with your other brother?" Landon teased.

"You know Blake and I are not cool. Don't even go there."

I agreed to go with him to the mall. He agreed to go study with me at the library first. Of course staying at Coach Strong's house, I couldn't just come and go as I pleased, but when I told Coach what I was planning on doing, he

was with it. He did give me a time to be back home though. That was fine with me because it gave me a reason to make sure Landon did not have me out all night.

Amir was one of the tutors. When I got there, he was not helping anyone. We had some of the same classes. We were just sort of getting to know each other really well. He was new to the football team, but the boy could ball. He was a free safety who could play his side, the strong safety position, and clear cross on the other side too. For depth purposes, if we needed him to play wide receiver, he was capable of that. Coach Strong said he was going to look at putting him in to catch the deep ball on special teams. The little joker had speed.

When I saw Amir sitting there ready to help others, something inside of me kicked in and I thought, "Dang, Leo, you got to get yourself together so that you won't be so dumb." There was no way I could afford to repeat a grade. I had already been there and done that. My dad passed when I was in the third grade. I was out of school for a long time because of our accident. I was already older than most, and I knew to be able

to play at D1 schools I was going to need better grades than I had. So I was ready for Amir to teach me.

"All right, so talk to me about which part you are missing," Amir said when we opened up the math book.

I looked at him like, *All of this doesn't make any sense. I don't get why you asking me specific questions. Aren't you the tutor? Give me some problems. Let me try and answer 'em. If I can't, help out.*

I do not know if I was too prideful or if I was too slow in the subject, but I really could not tell him what I did not understand. I was real frustrated. Thankfully, somebody sat on the other side, and he started helping that person.

"Look, man, I'm trying to help you," Amir turned and said once the other girl was working on some problems. "Take a break or something. Come back with the right attitude. You can get this. No need for drama."

"Aight, man," I said, really mad at myself because I did not understand it.

When I got up to get some water, Ella came rushing past me. She went in the back of the

library. I had never seen her so upset. She was shaking and crying. Instantly, I knew I had to be with her and calm her down.

Then I hesitated. It had been a week, and I had not told her how much I appreciated her. I had to open up. I had to be transparent. I had to be there for her because clearly she was going through something deep.

It took me a while to find her. I saw her on the ground with her knees to her face and her arms wrapped around them. She was crying hard. I bent down and hugged her.

"What's wrong? Talk to me, Ella."

"Oh, Leo," she cried, hugging me real tight.

I was way taller than her, so I leaned down and put my face to hers. Even though her face was wet from the tears, it felt nice rubbing up against her. I did not know what she was saying as she rambled. Trying to calm her down, somehow our lips connected. There in the library we ended up on top of each other. I actually wanted time to stand still. Ella felt so good in my arms.

"You don't have to take pity on me," she said, thinking I was not feelin' her.

"Pity on you? What are you talking about?"

She wanted to get up, so I moved off of her. "I'm a basket case right now, Leo, okay?"

"I'm here because I wanna be. I kissed you because I wanted too. If you trust me, talk to me."

"I'll run you away. My life is so crazy right now."

"Join the club," I said, letting her know I understood.

"It's my dad. He's getting married, and my stepmother-to-be hates me. Maybe she's jealous of me. I don't know, but she doesn't want me in her house. All I wanted to do was just spend time getting to know my dad, you know? It seems like I'm in the way."

"How do you know this?" I asked, wanting to make sure she wasn't stressing unnecessarily.

Not that I did not believe her, but sometimes girls had the tendency to exaggerate. I wanted to make sure what she *thought* was going on was really that. So maybe if she told me everything that happened, I could confirm her suspicions or let her know she was overreacting.

"I walked in on their conversation," Ella blurted out as evidence to support her theory.

She and I really did have a lot in common. I knew exactly how it felt to walk in on adults talking about you—and not in a comforting way. She was right to be feeling uncomfortable.

"I just don't feel loved. I just feel like it would have been much better if I didn't even try to get to know him. But he's my dad, right? He should care about me. He should wanna be there for me. He should wanna love me."

All of a sudden, when she said she did not feel loved, I wanted to let her know that there was somebody standing right in front of her who cared. I felt something really deep. I picked her up and put her against some books in that library. Our tongues collided and all was right with our world.

Until we heard Dr. Sapp. "What in the world?"

Trouble found me, and it was becoming more than I could bear. I certainly did not want to go back to ISS or worse. I definitely did not want to get Ella back in trouble. I guess he knew that Ella and I needed the moment and needed more of his grace because he gave us another stern lecture instead of tougher consequences.

After the "Don't let me catch you again" speech, he sent her on her way and grabbed my arm. "All right, Steele, you are pushing my patience. You fight in my school. Squat in my school. Bring the police to my school. Now you are trying to get busy in my school."

"Nah, nah, Doc, it wasn't like that," I blushed and said.

"Whatever. Again you can't be doing all that. What you were doing was over-the-top. Both of you are too vulnerable right now. Chill out, dang," he muttered, hitting me on the back of my head.

He loved doing that. Was I being a knuckle-head? Was I letting my desires lead Ella down the wrong path? I wanted to be good for her. Maybe I did need to slow my roll.

"I got you, Dr. Sapp."

"You got me?" he questioned. He stood there with his hands folded.

I knew Dr. Sapp was disappointed in me. Everywhere he went the last couple of weeks, he found me in a tough predicament. However, because he got in the mud with me, sort of understood where I was coming from, and did not

chastise me for my unfortunate circumstances, I wanted to do right by him. I wanted to do much better for myself too, of course, but I just did not want to let him down anymore. Seriously, I was sick of being a magnet for trouble.

I could still feel Ella's lips on mine, and I wanted to say something sweet to her. But she was already gone. The tutoring session was over, and I couldn't get outside quickly because everyone was exiting the building.

But then I spotted the prettiest sight I had ever seen: Ella waiting on a ride. I eased up behind her and put my hands around her waist. I whispered in her ear.

"I really liked that. Hope you're not mad. I hope you don't regret it," I said.

"Darn," she said.

I wondered, why the "darn"? I was a little confused. Then I saw she was frowning at the car that was pulling up to get her.

She turned around toward me and said, "Out of all the things going wrong in my life, you are what's right."

Then the smile vanished. She huffed before getting into the car with a lady. Before the car

pulled off, a little boy in the back was waving at me. I noticed it was her little brother, Evan. I waved back. Now I knew why Ella had such a long face. She had to ride with the soon-to-be stepmom that she heard lobbying for her to leave.

Landon patted my back real hard and pushed me toward his ride. "To the mall we go," he said.

I was so tired, and I did not get much studying done. I knew exams were going to be next week in some of my classes. I was not prepared. The mall was the last place I needed to be. A deal is a deal though. I told him I would go with him to the mall, so hopefully, we could swoop up something quickly, and then he could drop me off at the Strong's house.

"So wassup? You like Eva's sister?" Landon asked. I shrugged my shoulders. "Puleeze," Landon teased, "don't even give me that."

"Then why you asking me?" I asked.

" 'Cause I thought you and I were gonna be playas for life, that's all. Now you trying to settle down on me and stuff, getting all serious with one girl. I ain't gonna have my road dog no more. Amir and Brenton already tripping. Can't go five

seconds without being henpecked. Hallie wants me to do that, and Charli wants to do this," he teased, mocking our boys.

I had to laugh though. "I ain't gonna be like that."

Landon replied, "Yeah, right." When we got to the mall, he slapped two twenties in my hand. "My dad wanted me to give you this."

"Man, I can't take this, and your dad didn't want you to give it to me."

"You know Pastor King can shell out some loot to the needy," Landon kidded. "He heard about your story, and there's more coming. You know our church has got plenty of resources. So take it before I go buy me a new shirt with it."

Actually, that was a good idea. Having Ella in my life, I wanted to look nice for her. Also, I was hungry.

"I really appreciate it, Landon. You keep showing me that you're my brother. You aight," I said to him. I gave him a cool hug.

"You know I know that," he teased back with his arrogant self.

He loved talking about Blake having a big head, but his head was just as inflated. Who

could blame him? His dad had one of the biggest Baptist churches in the South. I knew it was hard not having a dad in your life anymore, but I also saw firsthand being with Landon that it was no picnic having a dad who was rarely around either.

We agreed we would meet up in the food court in an hour. As soon as we got inside, I wanted to call him and tell him to make sure he only spent an hour shopping and doing his thing because Coach gave me a curfew. However, I realized I left my cell phone in his car, which I did not feel like going to get. If it were any other person, it would not have been worth going back because for sure the car would have been locked. Landon was such a scatter brain. He got so excited about hanging out that he sometimes did not lock his car.

Continuing in the mall, I went shopping. I found a shirt that would show off my muscles. I figured Ella would like that.

I was on my way to the food court. Passing by the toy store, I saw little Evan. I did a double take when I saw him standing there crying his eyes out.

I bent down and said, "Evan, it's your buddy Leo."

"Leo. Football. Yeah," he replied, settling down a little.

"Where's your mom and sister?"

"Football," Evan responded. He seemed happy to see me and wiped his eyes.

He took my hand and dragged me inside the toy store. I hoped Ella was in there. I saw the lady she was with, but I didn't think I'd remember her. Certainly Evan would know his mom, so we searched.

He wanted a football. I found a Nerf one for three dollars. I purchased it.

Seeing him smile, I took his hand and said, "Let's go find Ella."

After searching for a while, I got real nervous. She had to be going out of her mind wondering where her little brother was. I was determined to find her right away.

"Let's play football," Evan said.

"Okay, let's try to find Ella. Then we can play football. All right, lil' man?"

The only thing I could think of to do was to get my cell phone from the car. I was hoping

Landon had not locked it. I wished I knew Ella's number by heart. I would have used the phone in the store, but I didn't. I did not know any of the people in the mall to trust leaving Evan with until I got the phone. We weren't parked that far from the door, so we walked outside.

I did not get five feet when I heard some cop say, "Put your hands up. Step away from the boy."

Another cop grabbed Evan. He started crying. I was really irritated.

"Put him down," I screamed.

The officer snarled and said, "You, put your hands behind your head. You're under arrest."

"What for?" I questioned.

"For kidnapping," the cop said to me, getting a little rough and wanting to show that the law was bigger and stronger.

That was a joke because if I wanted to flex my muscle, I could have gotten away easily. However, I had not done anything wrong—and they had guns.

"This is all a misunderstanding," I said.

"The mother of this boy has reported him missing. You're taking him out of the mall, which is illegal," the officer said to me.

I tried to explain what was going on, but I was being jerked all around. Cops were man-handling me like I was a sexual predator. I was actually glad they turned me around and took me back in the mall instead of to the police car that was out front.

When little Evan saw his mom, he rushed to her. I felt horrible seeing his mother's devastated face. I knew she was sick with worry. I looked for Ella. I did not want any of this to blow up and be a big deal. However, I could not find her. At least now Evan was okay. Ella's dad was there too. Once I spotted Ella, I could see that she was mortified when she saw me in handcuffs. Trust me, that was not the way I wanted her or her father to see me.

I finally tried to explain that I was just going to get my cell phone. They told me that I should have gone to mall security with Evan. When they asked Ella why she was so sure I was not trying to kidnap the boy, her answer surprised me.

"Because he's my boyfriend. I trust him completely," Ella said boldly.

"And, sir, you're okay with her boyfriend having your son?" the officer asked Ella's dad.

Her father said, "Yes, Leo is a fine young man."

Immediately, they took off the cuffs. I so wanted to pull Ella into my arms and hug her. I was her boyfriend? Though I wasn't complaining, I was shocked. She was serious enough with her feelings that she said them out loud. I was overwhelmed. I hoped I would not let her down, because to disappoint her would be more than she deserved.

"Dang, man. Handcuffs? What just happened to you?" Landon said after everything was over.

"C'mon, guy, let's get out of here," I said to my partner.

Though I was hungry, the mall was the last place I wanted to be. When we got out to his car, I laughed. His car door was locked. So even if I had reached his vehicle, I still would not have been able to get to my phone. Of all the times I needed Landon to *not* be responsible, he was.

"Blake's been hitting up my phone trying to figure out where we were. He said his dad was coming down real hard on him about his game," Landon remarked. "Dads kill me."

I did not respond because I wished I was in either one of their situations. My dad being alive to fuss at me would be a joy. Neither Blake nor Landon could comprehend that their lives could be much worse if their dads were absent.

Landon saw that I thought he was tripping and said, "Why you looking like that? Like we're not supposed to get mad when our folks get on us? I know it ain't good to say, but you got it good. Your dad's gone, just saying."

"Boy, please. Don't even insult me with no foolishness like that. When adults fuss with you, at least they care enough to stick around. My dad's dead, and my mom has abandoned me. I have no parental support. I have no one bothering me and being overbearing with me."

Landon put his hands on my shoulders and said, "Yeah, but sometimes it's just over-the-top. And they need to chill and let us make our own mistakes. At least you got an angel up there looking out for you."

I just nodded. The thought of my father up in heaven looking down on me gave me pause. Was I living my life in such a way that he would be proud? I knew the answer to that was no.

Yeah, I gave my all on the football field, but I was not giving my all in the classroom. Shoot, socially I had some issues too.

When we got to the Strong's house, we did not see Blake's car. Landon texted him. Blake was such a drama king. He knew we were on our way, so where did he go?

When Landon did not get an immediate response, he said, "He should be pulling up any sec. He said we were gonna hang out and do something."

"Blake ain't trying to hang out with me," I said to Landon.

Landon read earlier text messages from Blake. "He said the party already started. That is code for he has already had a lil' nip. Trust me, he's ready to hang out. Right about now his dad thinks more of you than he does of him. His ego is a little bruised."

"Like I made his dad compliment my game over and over and over."

"Just let's wait," Landon said, and he got out of his car.

We walked into the garage. I had no idea how true those words I spoke to Landon were. I

did not step six feet into the Strong's house before Blake's mom had an empty rum bottle that she held upside down and square in my face.

Mrs. Strong ranted, "Leo, this is absolutely unacceptable. I did not think I had to tell you that you are not supposed to be drinking. I know you are not my son, but you are in my home. I have rules."

"But, Mrs. Strong, that's—" Landon said before I grabbed his arm to hush him up. I just let her continue to fuss at me. Obviously, Blake was having some type of meltdown, feeling like I just stepped on his turf. Though I did not want his mother to think I was a bad kid, it was best. With all she was going through, I knew it would be worse for her to deal with if she knew the truth—that her son was the lush.

She continued scolding. "You're really gonna have some explaining to do when Coach Strong comes in, young man, because this is not okay. I know you got a lot going on right now, but alcohol is not the way to solve your problems. It only makes them worse."

She was so heated. Finally, she turned around and left. Landon looked at me like his eyes were

about to pop out. He was jumping up and down like he was trying to bust through the floor.

"Just hold it in. She don't need to know it wasn't me," I said to my boy.

"Whatever. It was a full bottle. He chugged it all."

"We better find Blake," I said, knowing he was not a heavy drinker.

"I do agree with you on that," Landon said.

He kept calling Blake, but he did not get an answer. I called Brenton and Amir to see if they had seen him. They had not. We thought maybe he went to the school to watch film with his dad, but we drove in the parking lot and only saw the coaches' cars out there.

"You better go in there and explain to Coach Strong what's going on. You didn't wanna hurt his wife's feelings, but his son is somewhere drunk."

"It's just fine," I said, knowing for me it was not, but I would have to deal with that later.

"The way Blake's been treating you, I can't believe you are standing up for him like this."

Thinking out loud I said, "I know how scared I was when I thought my dad was dying. Before I actually knew he was not going to make it at

all, I was unable to breathe. It's just a lot. I can only imagine that he is truly frightened about losing his mom. Being scared is making him do all kinds of stupid things. As his teammate and friend, I want to be there."

Landon nodded. We continued searching. I remember he was on-and-off dating this girl named Jackie on the dance team. I had her number and thankfully she answered.

"Hey, Jackie. This is Leo."

"Wassup, guy? You know some of my girls think you got it going on, out there doing your thing on the football team, and handling the Axes too. Everybody thinks you're the man. My problem is, two of my girls like you. I can send you pictures, and you can let me know which one you wanna go out with."

"No, no, no, I'm straight."

"Playa Leo is straight. I tried to tell them you didn't want just one girl, but they think they can settle you down," Jackie said, misunderstanding me.

"Look, I'm not calling about any of that," I said, moving on. "I'm trying to see if you hooked up with Blake today. Y'all still kickin' it, right?"

"You know your friend. I was supposed to be seeing him, but he didn't make it over here."

"How long ago was that?"

"Long enough for him to be here."

"Really?"

"Yeah, it's been like two hours."

"Aight, well, hit me back if you hear from him," I urged.

"You're not worried or anything, are you?" she asked.

Not wanting her to panic too, I said, "No, no, I'm just trying to connect with him."

"So I can tell my girls they gotta shot," Jackie diverted back to that.

"Nah, I'm off the market," I said, wanting to be clear.

"What? Who snagged you?"

"Ella Blount," I said proudly.

"Not one of them doggone cheerleaders? Please tell me no."

"See, why you hating on the cheerleaders?"

"They think they are all that, that's why."

"I'm just tired of the beef," I said, really wanting people to stop the drama. "Can we all just get along for real, for real?"

Jackie paused and said, "I hear you, as long as you're happy. Wow, Leo Steele is settling down."

"I know, right?" I said. "Remember to call me if you hear from Blake."

When I got off the phone, I told Landon that she did not know where he was. I also explained that she said he should have been over there a long time ago. We both got knots in our stomach.

"I'm worried, man," I admitted.

"Yeah, me too," Landon said. It started getting dark.

We drove everywhere. We went back to the Strong's house and retraced the drive from Blake's to Jackie's house. There was a steep hill along the route. We saw tire marks in the road, so Landon immediately pulled over and parked the car. Seeing the missing railing made us both clutch our hearts in fear. We looked over the edge and were horrified. We saw Blake's car smashed into a tree at the bottom of a hill. Just the thought that our friend might be gone was too much.

CHAPTER 5

Firmly Secure

Landon and I took off like we were running a race. Whatever our best times in the forty were, at that moment I know we both beat it in the mad downhill scramble. We knew every second was important to get to our friend, who had literally gone off the deep end.

"He's moving," Landon yelled out.

The front passenger side was smashed into the tree. The back passenger side and the whole driver's side were untouched. We tried opening the door, but it was locked. Landon and I banged on the window to get Blake to let us in.

"If he doesn't wake up, I'm going to bust this window out," Landon shouted. We were both frazzled.

"No, no, he's coming to. Besides, the glass might cut him," I said. Blake's head turned toward the two of us.

"Blake, unlock the door!" Landon called out. Blake complied.

When Landon opened the door, Blake's body fell toward us and I caught him. He was conscious, barely though.

"Where am I? What's going on? What's happening?" Blake asked, clearly out of it.

"Let's get him away from the car. With that kind of impact, this thing could explode," I cried.

Neither of us were doctors, but we knew how to check for signs that a body was in good working order. Since football was such a violent sport, we all kept each other in check. Thankfully, Blake had no bleeding, but he did have a knot on his forehead.

"He could have a concussion. We need to get him to the hospital," I said.

"No, no, ouch, no," Blake said, coming to. "What happened?"

Landon replied, "You were drinking. You drank a whole doggone bottle of rum."

"Oh yeah, I had a few nips," Blake said, trying unsuccessfully to stand. "I just need to get home before my parents trip."

"Why would you do this, man?" Landon asked.

Blake responded, "Why do you care? You've been all over my case, like I'm the worst."

"We both care, all right," I said to Blake, not needing him to work himself up. "Just stay with him. Let me check the car."

One of the cheerleaders, Hallie Ray, had a real cool dad who allowed me to work with him a couple of summers ago. I did not know everything about cars, but I definitely could tell if one was leaking fluids. It was like a time bomb waiting to explode. Blake's car passed all of the tests other than the impact the front right side took colliding with the tree. The car appeared to be working.

I looked behind me. There was no way we could get it back up the hill. A few feet below was another road. I went back over to Landon and Blake and explained to Landon what I was

thinking. He told me where the road went, and we got Blake in the car. I drove.

"I'm sorry. Ouch." Blake said, touching his ailing head.

"We really need to get you to the hospital."

"If I die, so what?" Blake said, sounding stupid.

"What's up with you, man? You got everything. You're the quarterback of our team, you got the looks ladies love. Your parents love you, and you're smart as heck. Why are you tripping?"

"You wouldn't understand. Everything comes easy to you."

He had to have a concussion because he was making no sense. Everything came easy to *me*? Please. I had nowhere to live. What was he talking about? I wanted to go off on him and say, "Why do you get jealous when your dad sings somebody else's praises? He's our coach, and he's a doggone tough one too. If he doesn't offer a compliment, it means we sucked."

We were 4–0. Blake needed to get his act together because some of the teams we had to face down the line were overpowering. We

certainly needed our quarterback to have his head in the game. As soon as we pulled up to his house, his mom came rushing outside. I knew at that moment Coach Strong was not far behind. They were like a pair of cleats. One was no good without the other. Sure enough, he came from the garage and freaked out when he shined the light on the damaged car.

Coach yelled, "What in the world happened to the car?"

"Oh my gosh, Blake, we need to get you inside right now, and I'm calling Doctor Parker. Bradley, you deal with him," Mrs. Strong demanded, pointing at me.

"Leo, what is going on, young man? I bring you into my home, and it's one thing after another with you, guy," Coach declared.

Why were they asking me what happened? Did they think their son was that freaking perfect that he was beyond getting himself drunk and crashing his car? But then I thought about it. The Blake he knew would not make such a stupid choice. Particularly a few weeks back when Blake was caught with alcohol in his car

and went to jail. Coach Strong knows everybody and had a friend in the police department who scared Blake straight, or so he thought.

When Blake got out of jail that night, he told all of us that he wanted no part of trouble and that he was never going to make that mistake again. That is probably why Coach Strong assumed it was me. What really hurt is that he gave me a look like I disgusted him. I did not deserve a medal, but I did not deserve to be shaken either. Soon, very soon, I'd be gone.

In chemistry class I noticed Ella was not herself. There was no smile was on her face, and she was keeping to herself. When the teacher asked us to do a lab, she was forced to talk to me since we were partners.

"Hey, you," I said. "I'm here, talk to me."

Dr. Sapp came over the intercom. "Hello, students of Lockwood High, a severe thunder storm is headed our way. All afternoon practices are canceled. Thanks and back to the books."

I asked Ella if she needed to talk. She studied my face and saw I was ready to handle whatever she wanted to throw at me. This girl

had my heart and it was breaking seeing her somber.

Finally, she said, "I've got some money. Since we don't have practice, there is a hotel down the street. Can you meet me?"

The Strongs hated me. I had no desire to be where I was not wanted. I would tell Coach I would be home later. Shoot, it wasn't his business to know my every move. Actually, he'd probably be happy that I wouldn't be there.

I gladly agreed to meet her. I could not wait for the day to be over. If I could have taken her right then and there on the shiny lab table, I would have. Ella had worked her sweet way into my heart and affected me greatly.

Ella texted me the room number. When I walked through the door, she instantly hopped on me, put her lips to mine, took off my jacket, and then raised up her shirt. She was beautiful. We made our way over to the mattress. I was on top of her, and things were heating up. Bad as I wanted her, I stopped. She was moving too fast. While I wanted to be her first, I wanted her to have no regrets.

"Is something wrong with me?" she asked.

"Ella, you are stunning. All I have been thinking about is knocking boots with you. Now that I'm here, I see you are vulnerable. You are shaking. Your first time should not be like this. What's wrong?"

Ella broke down and cried. "My dad's wife-to-be told me to leave their home. I was just getting to know him, Leo. She gave me money to go."

I held her. Wanting her to know she wasn't the only one with deep issues, I told her my woes. I explained that I'd been homeless because my mom moved to New York to be with a thug.

"How could she? You have no job. Where did she expect you to go? Gosh," Ella said in a furious tone. "We both understand selfish parents."

Opening up completely, I said, "I have never had a girl who has cared for me like you do, Ella. I want to be here for you. You called me your boyfriend and saved me from going to jail. You went out on a limb for me."

"I know. That was pretty risky, huh?" she joked. "I did not even give you a chance to let me know if you really wanted us to be an item."

I could tell she felt bad for asking me to be her boyfriend instead of the other way around.

To ease her mind, I asked her to be my girlfriend. She smiled and I kissed her gently. I brought her body to mine. We embraced and fell asleep.

About thirty minutes later, I woke up. My life decisions were weighing heavily on my mind. One thing I needed to change was my bad study habits. I had a couple upcoming tests and needed to be ready. I got up and started studying. It did not take me long to get frustrated. I grunted. Unfortunately, that woke Ella up.

"Math giving you issues?" she asked.

"I didn't mean to wake you," I said.

"You should have. Let me help you study," she responded.

Remembering Dr. Sapp telling me to allow her to help me, I did not resist. Normally, having her sitting on my lap would have distracted me. However, she was a very good teacher, and I was getting the math.

"I get it," I said after we did a few problems. "Let me do a couple more."

I was pumped that I was getting this. Ella told me she knew I could do it. It felt good breezing through problems. This was a sign I just needed to apply myself.

After we studied, we talked, ordered pizza, and fell asleep with our clothes on. About eleven o'clock, I felt Ella moving around. She was pretty restless. I understood. It was hard to relax when so much in your life was unsettling.

I wondered if Coach was going to be angry that I had not shown up. Was my mom even wondering about her son? How could I get Blake some help? Yep, hard to sleep when so much rambled around in the brain.

Now I had a girlfriend. I had to protect her. I wanted to provide for her. If we could live in this hotel room, life would be simple. Problem was, neither one of us had a job.

Ella tried to quietly get out of the bed. Putting my woes aside, I wanted to be there for her. I held on to my girl.

"You okay? I'm not too heavy, am I?" I asked. "Wait, are you crying?"

Upset, she sniffed, "I'm okay."

"No, you're not."

Ella said she wanted to be there for me. She asked me what was going on in my world. Guess I was fidgeting too. I opened up and told her about Blake's car accident and that the Strongs

had accused me of leading their son down the wrong path.

Ella defended, "What? What did you have to do with Blake's crazy ways?"

"I know, right? They didn't tell me not to come back, but I gotta figure out something else. I just wish I could take care of you," I said, hugging her.

We both lay still. I knew we were deep in thought over what was next for us. Life was hard. Now I knew why Dr. Sapp preached about having an education so much. I needed to make something of my life so I would not have to scramble all of my days.

Ella exclaimed, "We need to get food stamps and subsidized housing."

"Don't be silly."

"We can figure this out. We can't go back to the school and squat. I ruined that by letting Coach know what you were doing," she said in a gloomy tone.

"You *saved* me by letting Coach know. I'm going to college on a football scholarship one day, and you're going on an academic one. We can do this. We'll figure out a way to hold on. I'ma go to

the front desk and see if they have any tooth-paste and toothbrushes 'cause I want a kiss," I said, hopping up. I put on my kicks and rolled out the door.

I texted Coach and wrote, "Wanted to let you know I was good. No need to worry. I'll be getting my things out tomorrow."

Soon as I hit send, I wanted to rescind my action. Where would I go? Landon was my only option, but would his parents let me stay there?

When I got back to the room, Ella played her messages. Her parents were so worried. That warmed my heart.

I said, "You need to call your mom. And I can get outta here so she won't trip about me being here."

Ella hugged me and said, "No, you are going to be safe and stay here tonight. I can have her meet me down the street."

After we said our good-byes, I headed to take a shower. Honestly, I wished Ella was with me, though the thought of her reconciling with her mom was better. As the water rushed over my head and body, I hoped the plan of what to do next would rush over me too. I needed a total

cleansing in my life. Thankfully, I could crash in a safe place, even if only for one night.

I ended up taking a cab to the Strong's home. Coach was so disgusted with the hour I arrived that he simply let me in and went on his way. I tossed and turned all night. Being a guest in the Strong's house was the last thing I wanted. While being there was extremely comfortable physically, it was an emotionally tortuous situation. I had made the decision to put myself out of my misery, even if sleeping under a bridge was my only option. I was moving on.

Mrs. Strong was not making it easier when I smelled the delicious breakfast. I headed down to the kitchen, but I hoped she was not in there. I did not feel like being looked at in a demoralizing way any more. As I neared Blake's room, I was stopped dead in my tracks in the hall as I heard Coach Strong shouting louder than I'd ever heard him do in practice.

"Blake, I'm sick and tired of this, son. You have responsibilities. You don't do what's asked of you. Do you have a brain up there, son?" Coach shouted. He paused and continued, "Oh,

you gonna look at me and try me? Boy, I will jack you up, up in here!"

I do not know what Blake did not do. I just did not think a man should be yelling at his son so brutally. Maybe that happened a lot when I was not here. Maybe that had a lot to do with why Blake was engaging in destructive behavior.

Before I could get around the corner, Mrs. Strong rushed into her son's room. "Bradley?"

"Just stay out of this. I'm the one who has to make him a man," Coach said to his wife.

I was so sorry that I did not tell her that Blake was the one doing the things she had accused me of. It was clear that though I was in a beautiful house, this family had some ugly stuff going on, and I did not need to add to it. When I passed by Blake's room and saw that Coach Strong had his hand on Blake's throat, I rushed in and said, "Coach?"

Blake grabbed his things and ran by me. Coach did not say a word. He just looked at me like I was next but walked on past me, ashamed. Blake got in his rental car and drove away. Coach got in his car and drove away. Good thing the bus had not come. I certainly was not going to let

that good breakfast go to waste. I gobbled down some eggs, bacon, and French toast. Thankfully, I got outside just in time to get on the big, yellow ride.

At practice it was funny because Blake was going full speed. When the running back was running the ball, Blake was the defender and tried to take me out. Though he had muscles, the brother could not compete. One time he hit me so hard I wanted to pick him up by his knees and slam him down on his back. I thought about all the possible things rolling around in his head, but the knot that was still visible from his accident, so I just took what he was dishing out.

Coach Grey, the defensive coordinator, got in my face. "Why are you being weak? He doesn't have on the green flag. You can tackle him. The team we play this week may not be that good, but next Friday night that team has a quarterback bigger than Blake. What are you going to do then?"

"I'll be ready, Coach," I said, wishing he knew the whole story.

"Practice how you intend to play," Coach Grey shouted back.

When I saw Coach Strong looking on, I said, "I just don't feel like the bigger man should intentionally hurt a weaker guy."

I jogged back into position, hoping Coach Strong got the point. Everyone knew football was an aggressive sport, and to play it—probably even coach it—you had to be a little loony. Maybe Coach Strong needed to get some counseling. Though it was not any of my business, he did need to know how I felt about what I saw earlier. I really did not care what he felt about it. I had already planned to leave his house, and he needed me to be on his football team, so what could he do?

After practice Landon and I grabbed a bite to eat from Church's Chicken.

"You okay? Why are you quiet?" Landon asked.

We would always break down what happened at practice. We would talk about what our team needed to do to get ready for the upcoming game. We would be transparent with each other. But at that point, he could not see what was going on with me.

Tired of being too prideful, I just came out and said, "Look, I don't want to stay with

the Strongs anymore. Do you think your Dad would—"

"Yeah, man," Landon uttered before I even got the chance to finish asking. "I told you a long time ago that you could stay at my place. With Coach Strong's bipolar butt, you don't want to be around all those rules anyway."

"It ain't like Pastor King doesn't have rules," I said, letting Landon know I expected to adhere.

Being sarcastic, Landon vented, "Yeah, he's got them. He just isn't there to enforce them."

"Still, can you ask?"

"No telling when he'll be home."

"Let's call him right now."

"You want me to ask or are you going to ask?" Landon asked me.

"You know him. What's best?"

"I'll just ask him." Landon picked up his cell and called his father.

At the same time Landon was taking care of finding me a new place to live, I noticed the Axes were coming into the restaurant. Since I was not talking a lot, I was almost finished with my food. I could actually just throw away the box and jet out before trouble started. Landon was the slow

eater and had only eaten one of the three-piece mix he bought. He still had okra and half of his corn on the cob to gobble up.

I moved my fingers around in circles, giving him a sign to hurry the heck up. When I looked back over by the door where the Axes were, they disappeared. I heard laughs over my shoulder. I turned around, and they were right behind me.

"You ain't trying to leave, are you?" Shameek asked. Then he pushed me a little.

I stood up and towered over him. With everything going on, I think I was growing. I had to be six foot four now. Shameek was not at all petrified.

"Shameek, what's up, man?" Landon said with hype to try and deflate the tension.

I appreciated my friend so much, but him caring was moot. I could tell by the look in the faces of Shameek and all his cronies that he was not done flexing his muscles at me. As he bumped me, I knew he wanted trouble.

Frustrated, I said, "What, Shameek? What you gotta say? What, what do you want? What now?"

If I could just get him one on one, his tail would not come around me no more trying to act all tough. However, I had already learned that with twelve against one, odds were not in my favor, no day, no way. He had already flexed his muscles. He had already showed the world he could get the best of me.

"Bruno, what you think? Should I take him right here and finish what we started?" Shameek teased. "Come on, give me a reason. Hit me. Push me. You thought you were the man, stepping in the way of stuff that wasn't your business ..."

I just stood there. I was not going to let him get to me. I was not going to let him rattle me. I was not going to let him get under my skin.

Then he surprised me and said, "Or do I need to go take it from your little cheerleader?"

The Lockwood Lion came out of me at that moment because I practically roared in his face. I pushed him hard. Landon grabbed me and pulled me out of the way as the restaurant's security guard came toward us.

"How does he know about Ella?" I said to Landon as we got outside.

"Get in the car," Landon said. "Let's go."

There was no way I wanted something to happen to her. I was going to have to figure this out and fast. I needed Ella to be left untouched, never threatened, and firmly secure.

CHAPTER 6

Be Exact

As we pulled up at the Strong's home, I said to Landon, "So, you sure it's okay I stay at your place?"

"Yeah, man, I told you three or four times you're straight. What? The Axes thing freak you out? They make you scare-ed."

"That ain't funny," I replied, extremely bummed out that the tension with them was not over.

"Yeah, for real they are crazy," Landon said, realizing this was still serious. "You better warn Ella to watch her back."

"Yeah," I said, having that very thing at the forefront of my mind.

"Hurry up, though, it's Wednesday. My mom's making a good pot of spaghetti, and I want to be on time."

"You should eat faster. You wouldn't be hungry if you'd have eaten all that chicken," I said.

"Whatever, the Axes made me leave my grub. Them suckers probably eating it now. Besides, I looked up a bunch of D1 prospects. I need to put more meat on my bones, you know?"

"Do your thing."

"I'm just hoping when we play basketball, I won't run off all the weight I put on, you know?"

"Right, right. All right, I'll be right back," I assured.

I dreaded going up to the Strong's home. I wished I had money to get flowers to thank Mrs. Strong properly for allowing me to stay at her place. Hopefully, just the thought that I was leaving would make her day.

I rang the doorbell and Lola let me in. She wanted to tell me about her day. The girl could talk. I did not want to be rude, so I listened. Thankfully, her mom called her, and I was able to get to the guest bedroom and pack up.

A part of me just wanted to walk out and call Coach Strong later and say, "I'm gone." But my mom had raised me better than that. I owed the family a formal thank you and good-bye. Blake was not home. His car was still in the shop, and his insurance was so good that he was driving a rental. The brother had not missed a beat.

When I walked into the family room, I saw Mr. and Mrs. Strong watching the news. Lola was doing her homework.

I said softly, "Excuse me. Can I interrupt you for just a second?"

"Yeah, Leo, what's going on?" Coach asked.

"I wanted to thank you two for allowing me to stay here. I feel like it's time for me to go now."

Coach immediately stood to his feet. "Leo, you don't have to leave. Where would you go?"

I wanted to shout out, "Like you really care." But I knew he did care. He had opened his home to me. While it was not fair to get accused of the things I did not do, I did not blame Coach and Mrs. Strong. Just then, I heard a door slam and knew Blake had returned

Deep down, I knew Coach Strong cared. His eyes said he felt bad about my decision. I was

just as surprised when his wife stood up and came to me.

Mrs. Strong said, "Coach is right, Leo. I know we've been a little hard on you, but you cannot run from things. I know that all too well."

"I know why he's running," Blake explained, cutting into the conversation. "He's leaving because you guys were harsh on him for things he didn't do."

"It's all right, man," I said to Blake, not wanting to put my boy in any tough spot. His folks thought I did some things that he did. I had already taken the rap for it. I was leaving. No need to make this worse.

"What are you saying, Blake?" his dad asked in a tone that confirmed he suspected his son.

"I took the money that went missing. I drank your stash and another whole bottle. I was driving drunk, and I wrecked my car. Landon and Leo found me. All I really remember is being home the next day and finding out that Leo took the rap."

"Oh, so you think it's okay for other people to get blamed for your dumb mistakes," Coach Strong yelled.

Mrs. Strong stepped to her husband and said, "Maybe your response is the reason why. He's acting out. I told you he's older now, Bradley. You can't just scream at him like he's two. And even then it would be abusive."

"Like he's gonna listen, Mom," Blake complained.

"Why did you tell them?" I whispered to Blake.

" 'Cause I was being a wimp. We got a game to win tomorrow night. I can't throw my best defensive player under the bus. You stood up for me time and time again. I just haven't done right by you. I got more balls than that," Blake confessed. "Listen, punish me in whatever way you want, but don't let Leo leave our house. The cold shoulder he's been getting from the two of your guys has no merit. You have been nagging, telling him to straighten up."

"Why did you have to do that, son? What's your problem?" Coach asked. "Drinking and driving? Didn't you learn?"

Ignoring his dad's question, Blake said, "Mom, I just told you part of my problem is me. And I'm not gonna blame you, Dad. I'm smarter

than that. I have really been trying to analyze myself. Honestly, I'm not dealing with this whole cancer thing well. I lost my girl to my cousin. Every time I turn around, every player on the team is doing way better in your eyes than me. I threw a couple interceptions just to see if you would change your mean tune and get behind me to motivate me in a positive way, but you still kicked me to the curb. It's like nothing I do is ever good enough for you. Drinking helped me cope. I gotta get it under control though, Dad."

Coach reached out and grabbed Blake so hard it made me cringe. Then he pulled Blake to him and hugged him really tight. It was an intense moment. I could not believe what I was witnessing. In that neat father-son hug, I saw bonding.

Mrs. Strong came over to me and apologized profusely. I told her it was all good, and it was not her fault. Part of me just wanted to leave, but she grabbed my bag and practically begged me to stay.

"You're good for my son. You're good for my husband. God sent you to our family for this time, and I'm not gonna let you go. You stood up

for my son because you didn't want to put more on me. Your mom has raised a fine young man. Leo, I'd be honored if you continued to stay with us. Could you do that? It would mean a lot."

"If that's what you really want, I guess I can," I responded. She hugged me tight.

When I was released from her embrace, Coach hugged me. Blake and I slapped hands. To feel wanted and a part of something—part of a family—felt good. I ran outside to tell Landon it was all good.

Stretching for the game, I noticed the cheerleaders warming up not far away. I did not want Ella to see me staring in her direction. However, I could tell she was sad. Ever since the confrontation with Shameek, I decided I'd pull away from her. While it killed me, I could not confirm Shameek's hunch that she was my girl.

I was going to have to actually break up with her, though, because she wasn't getting my hints. I walked the other way in school. I took extra long to come out of football practice. I did not return her calls. I wanted her to get angry at me so she would leave me be.

When I saw her walking toward me with Hallie and Charli, I knew something was up. This was going to be hard. She was forcing me to break her heart.

Brenton and Amir were stretching nearby. When their girls went to chat with them, I knew I had to deal with Ella. In frustration, I put my hands up in the air. I hoped she would turn around so I could get in game mode. She did not.

Looking pitiful, she said, "Okay, what's wrong, Mr. Steele? Clearly, you don't want to talk to me."

"I did not want to hurt your feelings, but it's best if I don't have a girlfriend right now. I thought this could work out between us, but I was wrong," I said, lying and desperately wanting to hold her close.

"I didn't mean to push you away," she cried. It was killing me.

She came up to me and put her hand on my shoulder pad and got on her toes. Tough as it was, I had to step back. She looked like I had kicked her.

Unsure if the Axes were watching, I said in a tough tone, "I gotta jet."

I felt bad seeing her cry. However, I could not comfort her. She meant more to me safe and apart than in my arms and hurt.

Amir caught up to me. "Okay, dude, Hallie could not stop talking about how you got her girl Ella all sad. I thought you liked her. What's up?"

"I do like her. Man, I think I love her."

"So why the distance? Getting a little smooch isn't going to ruin your concentration during the game," Amir joked, pointing at Brenton kissing Charli.

"It's the Axes, man. Shameek cornered me this week and said he might go after my girl. I can't keep Ella in my life. Staying with me could hurt her far worse than breaking up with me would," I explained.

"Wow, dude, I hear you. We just gonna have to watch your back."

"No, I have learned you can't get involved or they will come after you too."

"Well, that's my decision. Twelve fighting one ain't going down if I'm around," Amir said.

"You just get ready to whup up on this team," I replied.

We did not have our starting quarterback. Coach Strong felt that since the team we were playing was not supposed to be that good, he wanted to keep Blake out the game to make sure he rested from the concussion from his car accident. As we got ready to play, I could tell Blake was down.

I went over and said, "Blake, no worries on this game, man. You should rest up. That knot is not gone."

"I'm fine, Leo. My dad should let me play. He's just punishing me because I wasn't truthful and have made some dumb choices. He hates me."

"Blake, be serious, dude. That man is passionate, but that passion stems from love. He's on you hard because he wants you to be dominant. When I stayed in his office, I saw so many pictures on his desk of you playing ball from the last ten years. He had notes about how Blake made him proud here, and Blake did awesome with that. He loves himself some Blake."

"Really?" Blake questioned.

"Really," I said.

"Leo, thanks, man. And I am sorry about giving you problems. Jackie told me how worried

you were about me. That was before you even knew I cared for you as well."

"Teammates, right?"

"Brothers, man," Blake said, giving me dap. "Now cream this team."

Blake got his wish. The game went our way from the start. We kicked the ball off to them, and their kickoff returner fumbled the ball. Brenton scooped it up and ran it in for a touchdown. On their next possession, they got the ball on their ten yard line. I got three sacks in a row. On my last sack, I found the quarterback in the end zone. We got a safety.

Much of the first half went just like that. We were not playing a pee-wee team, but it felt like it. Ella's little brother, Evan, could have given more effort than they were.

At the end of the game, the score was 35–7. We killed them.

Ella startled me when she came out of nowhere and blocked my path to the locker room.

"You're the man. Don't punk out. Talk to me."

"Thanks, but I gotta go," I said, trying to run around her.

"I heard something about the Axes has you tripping. Why does that have anything to do with me? Why does that have anything to do with you?"

"Shameek is telling everybody it ain't over between me and him. He doesn't make idle threats. I don't want anybody around me, including the girl I really care about," I said. I put my hand on her soft chin. "I don't want them to think I'm close to you. They know there's more than one way to hurt me. Ella, if anything happened to you … you know what? Just stay away."

I hated to jog to the field house and leave her upset. However, I meant what I said. She had to stay away. She knew I still cared, and that had to be enough for now. Her safety depended on it.

"Leo," Ella screamed. "Leo!" But I ignored her and kept heading toward the locker room.

I passed Amir and Brenton. They both heard my girl sounding desperate. The Axes were crazy, and if she didn't know how serious this was, I did.

Turning to my boys I said, "Y'all help me out. Please talk to her. That gang is crazy. Brenton, you know that."

Brenton said, "Got your back. We'll get her to understand."

I *so* wished my mom was there. I wanted to talk to her and let her know I was frightened. Here I was grown in society's eyes, yet I was as fearful as a child was of the bogeyman.

I didn't see Coach heading my way. "Leo, what's wrong?" he asked.

I wanted to tell him nothing. I wanted to say life was all good. I wanted to tell him to send me home now so that I could not get in trouble. However, I stayed calm and realized I needed to tell the truth.

"Coach, I've been threatened by the Axes. I'm worried for myself, for Blake, and for my girl."

Coach put his hand on his head and then looked at me. "Okay, you need to talk to the police and report this right away. Also, what's Blake got to do with this? And when did you get a girl?"

"It just sort of happened and the Axes know. They want to come after her to get at me. I tried to break it off with her for her safety, but ..."

Coach Strong shook his head. "I can only imagine she wasn't letting you go."

"No, she wasn't, and I like her, a lot. I don't know what else to do," I said, looking to him for guidance.

"Well, the police working security in the stands can take your statement, and then I want you home right after you speak to them. We let this cool down. We add no fuel to this fire. You get me?" he asked. I nodded. "And Blake?"

"Oh yeah, well, that's how all this got started, Coach. Blake stood up to a guy who beat up a girl. When the guy pulled a gun on Blake, I stepped in."

"What? You boys, dang! Tell me you weren't packing?" he asked. I looked the other way. "Boy, you better not have a piece in my home."

"I don't, sir. My mom's boyfriend pawned it."

"Good. You and Blake have too much going right for you now. Some of these thugs have nothing. Stay out of their way and tell the cops all you know," Coach demanded.

Amir and Brenton came into the locker room. I motioned my hand for them to come over to me. Brenton shook his head.

I said, "What? You couldn't talk to her?"

Amir replied, "Yeah, we talked to her, and we pulled no punches, but she is strong-willed and doesn't think this is as serious as we think it is."

"That's foolish. She saw those jokers bashing my head in the other day. Dang it! She better go home right now," I declared.

Brenton said, "I doubt it. But if you go home, she probably will."

"I just told Leo to talk to the cops about Shameek and the Axes," Coach said. "I think you both need to do the same," he said, nodding toward Blake and Landon. They both agreed to go with me to talk to the police.

Coach then told Blake and me to head home without him. He was going to stay and watch film of next week's opponent. Waxton, our star running back, announced he was having an after party. The guys wanted to go. I hoped the cheerleaders were not planning to go.

When Blake and I drove to his place, Amir called me. "Hey, just wanted you to know the girls are going to Wax's gig. Not sure about Ella, but I know Hallie went."

"Thanks, Amir. Hopefully, she heard us and went home. I'll check," I said.

"If she went, what you gonna do?" Amir asked.

"Go drag her home, I guess. Hope I get there before the Axes do," I responded.

When I hung up, Blake said, "Maybe all this is much to do about nothing. The Axes like to have us worried. We're too high-profile, winning and all, for them to step to us."

Blake had a point. However, the Axes were not rational. Whether it was puff or real stuff, I had to take care of mine.

"You say the word, and we head to the party," Blake said, having my back.

"Let me see what's up," I said. I began to push letters on my cell.

I texted, "Please tell me that you are not out at Wax's place."

Ella responded, "Yes, but if you tell me where you are, I can get Hallie to drop me off."

I texted back, "Go home."

She texted back, "Soon."

Seeing that message, I gave Blake the signal to loop the rental around. Blake called Landon and I phoned Amir. If there was drama, we did

not want to be alone. I wished I had my gun, but it was what it was.

About fifteen minutes later, we pulled up to a crowded house full of teens. Most were getting their party on, but I panicked when I saw the Axes's cars. I had to find Ella. My gut told me she was in trouble.

Sprinting to the house was still not fast enough for me. If something happened to her, I could not forgive myself. When I was stopped by two Axes, who looked at me like I was too late, I freaked. I pushed my way past them quickly.

"Where is she?" I screamed.

"We'll find her," Blake assured. "Look, there's Charli and everybody."

I was so happy to see Ella's crew. I looked at all the girls, but I did not see Ella. Then I did a double take when I thought I saw her. However, it was her identical twin sister. I stepped to Hallie.

"Where's Ella?" I asked, knowing that she knew I cared.

"It's been a while since we've seen her," Hallie said.

I went around and called out for her, "Ella? Ella?"

When I didn't see her upstairs, a group of us headed to the back deck. Charli started crying, as my demeanor was making her nervous. Blake comforted her.

"She hasn't left because I'm driving," Hallie declared.

"Down—" I heard Ella scream before her voice was abruptly cut off.

I jetted down the stairs. Shameek was on top of Ella. My heart was racing.

"I wondered where you were. I was about to have fun and do what you haven't. You come to watch?" Shameek tormented. "You should not have interfered. You wanna be the hero with Blake Strong; well, now I got the last word."

"Shameek, let her go. Your problem is with me, not my girl," I said.

"Ahh, you told me you didn't have a girl. I got eyes and ears everywhere. Thought I couldn't find who the trick was that ratted us out when we were bashing your head in? Well, I did. Now I want to finish it," Shameek promised. Just then, Bruno tossed him over a gun.

Amir came down the stairs and yelled, "Leo, watch out!"

"No!" Ella shrieked. Then she ran in front of me.

My eyes popped when I saw the bullet head her way. I pushed her. However, she got hit.

"No!" I wailed. She fell, and I caught her and broke her fall.

Chaos went on around us. Amir and Landon grabbed Shameek. Ella was trembling and I felt sick. I held her close and tears fell.

"Stay with me," I begged. "Ella, stay with me. I love you, girl. Please, don't leave me. Call the ambulance! Somebody!"

Ella tried to speak, "I … I …"

She was with me, but she needed her strength. I tried to get her to stay calm. However, I was struggling with keeping myself together.

She tried to talk again. "Love … love …"

I said, "Shhh, don't speak … don't talk now."

"Love you," she whispered out. "Where … Eva?"

Knowing she wanted her sister, I responded, "Shhh, we'll find her."

Eva, wailing loudly, came through the crowd.

Why did she run in front of the bullet? Ella was lying helpless because she wanted to protect

me. But it was my job to protect her. Not since my dad made sure he protected me in the car crash had anyone ever made sure I was taken care of first. When I saw her eyes shut, I could only hope she was not gone from my life like my father was.

I had given my heart to her, and I needed her to stay around to receive my love. She needed to hold on, and she needed to be okay. She needed to live, to be exact.

CHAPTER 7

Completely Satisfied

It felt like my heart had been torn out of my body. All I wanted was for Ella to survive. However, all I could do was pace across the hospital waiting room.

I now had a deeper appreciation for how Ella must have felt waiting in the hospital when I was brutally beaten. She needed to make it so I could argue that my waiting was way worse. We weren't even, but now we were more connected. She felt like a part of me. It was making me crazy that I was not in her place. It should have been me.

Landon came to me and said, "Quit pacing, dude. The paramedics said thanks to you pushing her out of the way, it was just a graze. She's probably only getting stitches—if she even needs that. She ain't dead."

My eyes could not roll at him any harder. He needed to find love, and then he'd get this new feeling. I was worried beyond what I could explain. I breathed deeper and tried to collect myself.

Hallie came up behind me and said, "Leo, I am so thankful Ella has you in her life. When I first found out she liked you, I tripped. You have always been a playa and too cool to show any care about any one girl. But she's changed you. She is crazy about you, and clearly there is no denying you are into her as well."

I couldn't look at Ella's best buddy. I had a rep and now it was changing. It did not bother me that I was wearing my feelings on my sleeve, but I was slightly embarrassed that the tough defensive end who I was known to be was transforming into a teddy bear.

"I just want to see her and know she's okay," I muttered.

Hallie took my hand, pulled me close, and whispered, "This is déjà vu for me. When you were in here a few weeks back, Ella slipped back there. We can distract folks. Go now."

I was not as tiny and cute as Ella. I could imagine her avoiding the doctors, nurses, and hospital workers. A very tall black male was not as inconspicuous. However, where there was a will, there was a way.

After going into two wrong rooms, I landed in the right one. Ella was resting peacefully. I was happy to see she was not in pain.

While I avoided the staff, I forgot to factor in Ella's mom. She stepped up to me and went off. I just let her pound me in the chest. This was my fault.

She screamed, "You did this to her. What have you done to my baby?"

I replied, "Forgive me, please. I'm sorry."

Ms. Blount was not accepting my apology. "Get out. Ella doesn't need to be around you *ever*. You put my child in danger. She might not make it."

What in the world was she saying? I thought Ella did not have a serious injury. I knew I needed

to see for myself. Oh no, this was horrible. Turning to get out of there, a nurse was at the door. I could not move.

The nurse stepped around me and said, "Ma'am, your daughter is not going to die from getting grazed by a bullet. Let's not exaggerate."

"Then she is going to be okay?" I asked the nurse with hope in my voice.

The nurse smiled and said, "Yes, she's going to be just fine. She's a lucky girl."

Ella must have heard the commotion. She tried sitting up. Her mom went over to comfort her.

"Ella, baby. Oh, honey," Ms. Blount said, stroking Ella's forehead and fixing her hair, which I thought was perfect.

Ella mumbled something to her mom. I knew they needed their time. She didn't want me in there.

I said, "I'll let you talk."

Ella sat up and lobbied for me to stay. She told her mom she loved me. My heart started beating again.

"What?!" Ms. Blount said with her nose flared in disbelief.

I said, "It is fine, Ella. Your mom is right. You shouldn't have been involved."

Ella fought to speak. "Mom, Leo asked me to hang low. This is the guy we made the baskets for. The stupid gang members did this, not Leo."

Her mom grilled, "Then how and why did you get a bullet to graze your arm?"

"This guy was trying to shoot me, ma'am," I acknowledged.

"My point. Please, keep your distance from Ella," Ms. Blount verbalized.

Ella admitted, "Mom, I ran in front of Leo so he would not get shot. However, Leo was the real hero. He pushed me so the bullet wouldn't hit me. We were trying to protect each other."

My blood was boiling hotter than a pot does turned up high on the stove. Shameek had taken things too far. He needed to be stopped for good.

Trying to get Ms. Blount to understand this was a big deal to me and I'd handle it, I said, "Ms. Blount, I did not want any of this. However, please know I will take care of it."

"Listen, son, the police need to get involved and handle this," her mom preached.

Ella uttered, "Mom, no, because they will come after us."

"Too late for that. We are going to get the whole community to stand up against this meaningless violence," Ms. Blount cried passionately. "Leo, I'm sorry I was so harsh. Hitting you was uncalled for. Thank you for protecting my baby."

"No thanks needed," I said.

"Well, promise me you will stay away from that gang," she stressed. "Promise me, please. If you keep the feud going, you are no better than the thugs. Promise me."

"I promise," I finally agreed. She left to call some folks and check with the nurse. "Dang, Ella, I want to hug you. I don't want to hurt your arm though."

"Hold me," Ella said, her voice quivering a little. "My mom is right. You can't go after those guys, baby."

Hearing her call me baby made me grin. "I don't know what I would have done if they would have killed you."

She squeezed me, "I could not let them shoot you."

"You should have stayed back."

"No, I could not bear the thought of you being in the hospital again."

I stroked her cheek and said, "And you think this is a picnic for me seeing you in here?"

"Well, we are a match for each other. We can't keep trouble away," Ella teased. "I love you, Leo."

I kissed her forehead and said, "I love you too. You do my work. You get me food. You call the police. You step in the way of a bullet intended for me."

"Yeah, but you pushed me out of the way, and you're here to make sure I'm okay."

"I guess you're stuck with me."

The door opened, and I got up off the bed when her mom entered with two policemen. We were asked questions about the shooting and the assault. We were also informed that all our friends explained what the Axes had been doing. The idea that we could disband their group was reassuring.

"For now I have all I need. Miss, you are very lucky," the officer told Ella.

The officers vowed to get the Axes off the street. Ms. Blount said she was holding them to

do just that. I could see her at the police station every day following up too. Ella was blessed to have a mom who cared so much. It actually made me a little melancholy missing my own mother.

As Ella's mom showed the cops out, I bent down to Ella's cheek and said, "Rest up. I'll see you tomorrow for sure."

I kissed her forehead and went out into the lobby. Our friends were still waiting. Hallie, Amir, and Blake rushed up to me. They were happy to know she was truly all right.

Ella was in tears the next day when a bunch of us came over to her place to surprise her. "Wow, y'all did not have to come see about me!"

Everyone stood around her, but I found a place beside her on the couch. I put my arm around her. I had never been a romantic, but all I thought of was getting to her. Honestly, I wanted her to myself, but Charli, Randal, Hallie, Blake, Landon, Brenton, Amir, and her sister made it a party. My boys made me look bad, bringing Ella gifts. When I called them on it, Ella kissed my cheek to let me know that just my presence was a gift to her.

After Ms. Blount fed us all, Charli and Hallie rose to leave. Ella tried to get them to stay. I *so* wanted her to want to just hang with me. Everyone could have left us alone, and I would have been satisfied.

Charli whined, "I would stay, Ella, but I need to study for exams."

"Got you," Ella said, "I need to study as well."

Ms. Blount came into the room and said, "I heard the right word, studying. Good. Everyone has As, right?"

I was the last person who wanted someone to check on my grades. I had not applied myself this semester and the results were showing. Unless I scored an eighty or above in US History and math, I would get an F in those classes. Thinking about my situation got me down.

Ella walked most everyone out, but Randal and I stayed with her sister. The way Ella was smiling, I knew she was thinking something. I was not tuned in to her yet, so I had no idea what she was up too.

"Listen, big tests are coming up. I want to help you guys. I need to get some rest now, but tomorrow after church, let's study. All next week

after we are done with our practices, we'll study. If you all work with me, I promise you'll ace the tests."

I was not looking forward to cramming. However, I had no choice. I remembered Ella explaining math to me in the hotel. I could really follow her.

The week of Ella cracking the whip and making sure we studied hard was intense. She assessed each of us to see where we were weak. She then worked with us individually to connect the missing links. I was proud of myself for understanding it all. I was doubly proud of her for passing on her knowledge so effortlessly.

"You are an impressive teacher," I said to Ella after practice on Thursday. "Bring on the tests tomorrow. Thank you, Ella."

"No thanks needed. You buckled down and decided to do this. You want it, and you made yourself learn."

I replied, "I've always wanted to learn; my teachers just haven't been this caring."

Ella touched her arm. She didn't appear to be hurting. However, I had to make sure.

"How's that arm?"

"I find out tomorrow when I go to the doctor. I feel good though. The stitches just itch sometimes," Ella said. She scratched around the dressing. "What about Shameek? Do we need to worry about him?"

"No, baby, seven of the Axes were arrested. Two are in jail, and five are in juvenile detention."

Friday was a big day for me all around. I aced both tests, and since I did so well, I had a chance to get Bs. My teachers were so impressed that they were going to let me redo a few assignments. To get zeros erased would easily raise my grades.

Under the big lights of the football field, I felt that my dad could see me and approved of my performance. I hated that my mom wasn't there to see me do my thing. However, I kept my head in the game. I could not control her or be down because she made a decision to live in another state. No, I had to stay focused, stay in my lane, and worry about me. With Blake executing on offense, and the defense rock solid, we held the other team to three points. We scored twenty-five. Our pitiful kicker missed two of the

four field goals. We all hoped the new white boy would get eligible and save us in that area. If we were playing talented teams, we would need him to make extra points and field goals.

In the locker room, Coach Strong announced that he was so proud of us. We were into the second half of the season, and we were on a roll. We were still undefeated and doing everything in our power to stay that way.

Coach said, "Listen, men, I am overjoyed by your play. We always have a few things we can improve on. Special teams especially needs work. Tomorrow morning, let's watch film. Then for those who are free, plan to go to a cheer competition."

"A *what*, Coach?" Waxton huffed.

Knowing I was a leader on the team, I used my influence and said, "Dang, Wax, you heard Coach. Let's go support the cheerleaders. They cheer for us every week. Let's support them. What's up?"

Waxton said, "I heard you, doc. I'm in. It'll be nice seeing all those girls. Know what I'm sayin'?"

Lots of the guys gave him dap. I really didn't care why they decided to go. It would just be neat for the squad to have us there.

At the competition, Ella could not cheer because of her arm. However, I loved sitting in the stands with my girl. I had to keep her uplifted. I could tell she really wanted to be out there with everyone.

I was actually surprised that cheering was so intense. The teams were super good. When our girls stepped out and saw the support, they smiled. They also did their thing, flipping and stunting and jamming on the dance number.

The announcer called Ella to the center of the floor. She was so stunned. I helped her up to her feet.

"Ella Blount, on behalf of all the cheerleaders here today, we present you with a bouquet of roses. The violence you endured was gut-wrenching. However, we are thankful you are all right."

Many surrounded my girl. I was happy for her. I didn't know much about the sport, but I knew everyone wanted to win. For the other teams to be so caring was cool.

Our girls came in second place. Lockwood Lions fans let out joyous screams. Ella looked

over at me and I hit my chest. I had nothing but love for my girl.

"I'm telling you, Ella, your girls did great," I said into my cell. Amir was just dropping me off at the Strong's home. "Though they could've done better if you were out there with them."

"You're too good to me," she said.

"I'm just glad things are working out," I told her.

Her life was great at home. Since she moved back home with her mother and sister, and since the shooting, she had been feeling the love that she deserved to feel all along. She was such a sweet person, and I was happy that people were not playing with her heart.

As soon as I hung up the phone with Ella, my phone rang. It was Coach Strong. While Landon and Blake found it irritating to have someone checking on them, I was overjoyed.

"Hey, Coach," I said into the receiver with excitement.

In a strong tone Coach said, "Steele, where are you? I need to talk to you about something

real important. I don't need you to dilly-dally around after the cheerleading competition."

"I got you, sir. Amir is dropping me off right now. I'm in your driveway."

"Oh, okay, great. Come on in."

It was just a weird feeling I got that all was not right. Just when I thought everything was good, I had a sick feeling life was going to change. Things were too perfect. The Strongs were okay with me staying there. Blake and I were getting along like brothers. The Axes were dealing with the police. And my girl and I had each other. Now there seemed to be drama.

It could not have been my grades. We had just taken exams and I had done well on them. What was the problem now? Did Mrs. Strong change her mind? Did she want me to go? I hoped that was not the case because she had pleaded with me to stay.

Trying to stay cool, I took a deep breath. I did not want to second-guess the situation and stress myself out for nothing. I rang the bell and hoped I was wrong.

"Come on in," I heard Coach calling out.

I opened the door. Never in my wildest dreams could I imagine what he wanted. However, when I looked across the room and saw the face staring back at me, I was numb.

"Mom?" I called out.

She stood to her feet, rushed over to me, and threw her arms around me like I was the lost child she'd been looking for. I instinctively pulled away. I guess inwardly I was a little salty with the fact that I was here all the time, struggling for the last couple of weeks trying to figure out where to live and how to get food to eat, and she left me to do just that. Now she seemed sorry. Why?

"What's going on? Why are you here?" I said with attitude.

"Son, be respectful of your mom," Coach butted in and said.

I nodded. He was now like a dad to me. However, he could not make my distaste go away. I could not help that my heart was having trouble being warm to her.

"It was so nice talking to you," Mrs. Strong said to my mom. "We're going to let you two have some time. Bradley, come on."

She pulled her husband out of the family room. Clearly, he wanted to stay. Coach was an all right dude.

My mom could tell Coach was having trouble leaving, so she said, "Thank you both for taking care of my boy."

As soon as they were gone I looked at her and said, "Seriously, Mom, I don't mean any disrespect, but things are okay for me. What's going on? Why are you here?"

She rushed up to me and said, "I made a mistake. Leo, I shouldn't have left you, baby."

I turned away, but she grabbed both of my hands. "I'm your mom, but I'm also human. I know I'm supposed to make the wise, smart choices, but I didn't make one this time. I let this guy say all the right things to get me away from the only thing in life I care about, and that is you."

"What do you expect me to say, Mom? I'm stable right now."

"I know, I know. Coach said you can stay with him until I get myself together."

"And where you gonna go? It's tough out there being on the streets. I know, Ma, I've been doing it."

"There's a homeless shelter downtown that I'm able to go to."

"And we plan to help your mother get on her feet," Coach Strong interrupted. He and his wife came back into the room.

"The cancer center needs some nurse's assistants. I made a few calls, and your mom has an interview tomorrow," Mrs. Strong said.

"And I'm going to take your mom to the shelter and get her settled," Coach explained, sounding like I should be happy about all of this. "As soon as space opens up at this new apartment complex the government is funding, we'll get her moved in."

"You don't seem happy, Leo. What's wrong?" my mom asked, rightly sensing my distance.

"I just don't know, Mom. This is a lot. How do I know you won't take off again? Leave me? I know I'm supposed to be a man, but I'm still your son."

So many of my teammates hated their parents having short leashes on them. If they walked a day in my shoes, having no one care where you were, they would learn to appreciate what they had. Life on your own was no

picnic. I proved you could make it, so no one had excuses. However, having a silver spoon or parents there was a real boost to a great start in this hard life.

"And I care about you too, son. It was eating up at me. I know I don't deserve to ask for your forgiveness, and it may even take you a while to trust me again, but that's my mission. That's my goal. That's my aim."

"Leo, why don't you go and wash up for dinner," Mrs. Strong said, seeing my mom and I were at an impasse. "Mrs. Steele, please join us. I have plenty and would love for you to stay."

"No, thank you," my mom said to Mrs. Strong. I could see I had hurt her feelings. "Coach, if you don't mind getting me to that shelter, it looks like I've worn out my welcome here."

Coach reluctantly nodded. My mom walked over to me. She tried to give me a kiss on the cheek, but I was not feeling it. Coach wanted to sock me, but I had to be true to me.

I went and washed up, even took a shower to relax and think. The guilt of being too hard on my mother just kept eating away at me. For so long, all I wanted was for a parent to care. She

altered her whole life to come back and be with me. I was resisting.

My family was just the two of us. She was the last link to my dad. Right now I had the power to make us whole. I learned so much over the last couple of weeks. I knew education was the key to everything, and I was no longer going to be the class clown or the tough one and not get the knowledge that I needed to be successful. Just like I was working out my muscles, I also needed to work out my mind. It took Coach no time to come back. Over dinner I just played with my food. He kept watching me, and I hated that I was letting him down.

Finally, I said, "Coach, if you don't mind, can you take me to the shelter?"

"No problem at all. Let's go."

"You guys better eat first," Mrs. Strong suggested. I happily obliged because I was really hungry.

When I got to the shelter, my heart broke. Seeing people down on their luck was tough. Most, if you asked them, would probably admit they made bad choices; however, it was still not cool to see anyone struggle.

There were a bunch of cots. People looked like they had not bathed lately. However, they seemed to be good-hearted folks who just needed the shelter to help them turn things around in their lives.

The lady at the desk looked at me and said, "No visitors after eight o'clock."

I took the knapsack off my back and said, "No, ma'am. I'm here to stay. Do you have one more bed?"

"Just one more. You're lucky."

After walking around searching for ten minutes, I saw my mother on her cot, reading. I touched her back. She looked up and smiled real pretty at me.

"Leo, what are you doing here, son?"

"I came to be with you."

"No, you're not. You're staying with the Strongs. You don't need to be in here."

"Mom, I'm your son. Until I go off to college, wherever you go, I'm going. I love you, Mom," I declared.

"But you're gonna make me feel bad that I can't provide for you the way I need to. Let me just get on my feet. That big beautiful house

Coach has with his sweet wife is perfect. They want to take care of you. Look where I'll be for the next few weeks," she said, looking around at the humble place.

"Mom, having you back here wanting to take care of me is all I need." I gave her a big hug.

She was broken in my arms. Repeatedly, she said she was sorry. I let the tears I had been fighting go. I told her I was thankful. I was thankful for so much. Thankful that it worked out just the way it was supposed to. I had grown up since she left. I was thankful that this whole ordeal made me appreciate this life. I had the chance to make something out of nothing. Now my family was together.

I believed my dad was looking down on us, smiling wide, and happy we were trying. The love I felt in my heart and the conviction I had to strive hard daily and be the best me I could be, made me feel at peace. Though our life was a tad unstable, we had a roof over our heads, and we had each other. For those blessings, I was completely satisfied.

STEPHANIE PERRY MOORE is the author of many YA inspirational fiction titles, including the *Payton Skky* series, the *Laurel Shadrach* series, the *Perry Skky Jr.* series, the *Yasmin Peace* series, the *Faith Thomas Novelzine* series, the *Carmen Browne* series, the *Morgan Love* series, and the *Beta Gamma Pi* series. Mrs. Moore speaks with young people across the country, encouraging them to achieve every attainable dream. She currently lives in the greater Atlanta area with her husband, Derrick, and their three children. Visit her website at www.stephanieperrymoore.com.

DERRICK MOORE is a former NFL running back and currently the developmental coach for the Georgia Institute of Technology. He is also the author of *The Great Adventure* and *It's Possible: Turning Your Dreams into Reality*. Mr. Moore is a motivational speaker and shares with audiences everywhere how to climb the mountain in their lives and not stop until they have reached the top. He and his wife, Stephanie, have co-authored the *Alec London* series. Visit his website at www.derrickmoorespeaking.com.

WANT A DIFFERENT
point of view?

JUST *flip* THE BOOK!